FOX TALES

Tomihiko Morimi

FOX TALES

Tomihiko Morimi

Translation by Winifred Bird
Cover art by Gaku Nakagawa

Original Japanese trade edition published in 2006 by SHINCHOSHA Publishing Co., Ltd.
English edition published by arrangement with SHINCHOSHA Publishing Co., Ltd. through Tuttle-Mori Agency, Inc., Tokyo.

Yen On
150 West 30th Street, 19th Floor
New York, NY 10001

Visit us at yenpress.com • facebook.com/yenpress • twitter.com/yenpress
yenpress.tumblr.com • instagram.com/yenpress

First Yen On Edition: November 2022
Edited by Yen On Editorial: Emma McClain, Ivan Liang
Designed by Yen Press Design: Wendy Chan

Yen On is an imprint of Yen Press, LLC.
The Yen On name and logo are trademarks of Yen Press, LLC.

Library of Congress Control Number: 2022035999

ISBNs: 978-1-9753-3546-5 (hardcover)
978-1-9753-3547-2 (ebook)

10 9 8 7 6 5 4 3 2 1

LSC-C

Printed in the United States of America

CONTENTS

Fox Tales

The Dragon in the Fruit

Phantom

The Water God

Fox Tales

Amagi lived near Saginomori Shrine in Kyoto's eastern hills.

His old mansion sat at the top of a long, sloping street. Behind it was a bamboo grove in constant shadow, from which the sounds of rustling leaves never ceased to emanate. I visited Amagi's mansion for the first time on a windy day in early fall, running an errand for Hourendou, and I remember the bamboo grove writhing like a living creature as it began to sink into dusk. Towering there in the shadows, the stalks looked to me like enormous bones.

I passed through the sturdy wooden gate with the cloth-wrapped bundle Natsume had given me under my arm. Circling around to the garden as she had instructed, I paused before the stone step leading to the veranda and called out my greeting. Amagi emerged from a dark corner of the adjacent room. He was dressed casually in a bright blue kimono. He looked sleepy. His long, narrow face lacked vitality, the light stubble on his jaw giving it a bluish cast.

"I've come from Hourendou," I said, bowing my head.

"This way," he replied dourly and led me inside.

Every part of the mansion was dark. I learned later that Amagi didn't care much for lights. As we walked briskly down the long, cold corridors, I glanced up at him. The white gleam of his bony wrist protruding from the sleeve of his kimono seemed to float on its own through the darkness.

○

Hourendou is a curio shop in Ichijoji, not far from Saginomori Shrine. All sorts of secondhand goods were packed into that little room, the size of maybe six tatami mats. As Natsume had told me once self-effacingly, hers was no pedigreed antique shop. She dealt in anything old and interesting. That was why a university student like me, without any particular knowledge of antiques, was able to get a job there. Still, Natsume was in frequent contact with a number of Kyoto's distinguished old antique dealers and seemed to have some sort of connection to them that I didn't understand.

I didn't know Natsume's age, but I guessed she was a year or two past thirty.

I first met her when I was a sophomore at university. I had a job delivering bento lunches at the time, and I visited her shop on a delivery. As I slid open the glass doors, her bento in hand, there was a clatter, and she rose from the chair at the back of the shop. She was taller than me, with a kind look in her clear eyes. I thought to myself that she was a beautiful woman.

After that, I forgot all about her, but when I quit my delivery job at the start of junior year, I suddenly thought of her again and decided to stop by the shop. I didn't intend to buy anything, but in order to strike up a conversation, I think I asked her about one of the tobacco trays or netsuke figurines lining the shelves. After that, we started chatting. "I delivered a bento here once," I said. To my surprise, she remembered.

"I recall how cold your hands felt when I handed you the money," she said. She had a bit of a stiff way of speaking.

"It was winter, after all," I replied.

"That was the first time I ever had a bento delivered—and the last. Your hands must have been freezing. I felt sorry for you." She smiled apologetically.

There was a flyer on the door advertising an opening for a part-time assistant. I told her I'd recently quit my delivery job and wanted to try something more unusual. Smiling as if a weight on her shoulders had suddenly lifted, she said she'd love for me to have the job.

I began to spend my weekends at Hourendou in Ichijoji.

The work was simple. All I had to do was watch the shop and drive around to make deliveries. Natsume took part in several of the regular flea markets around the city, including one at Toji Temple on the first Sunday of every month and another at Kitano Tenmangu on the twenty-fifth. Several days beforehand, she would busily begin preparing her wares, and early on the day of the market, I would ferry them over in her van. Although she had a license, she was apparently petrified of driving, and she told me with a smile that she was very relieved to have me on staff.

○

I was led into a strange, unpleasantly long and narrow room. A leather sofa rested on the tatami mats covering the floor. On three sides, the room was enclosed by sliding screens decorated with bizarre illustrations. On the fourth side, to my left, were translucent paper *shoji* and, beyond them, what I guessed to be a garden. The paper on the *shoji* must have been changed very recently, because it glowed a bluish white, illuminating Amagi's face as he slouched lethargically on the sofa toward the back of the room. Because of the room's long, narrow shape, I felt as if he was terribly far away from me.

"Show me what you've got," Amagi muttered, taking an unfiltered cigarette the size of a pinkie finger out from a silver case and lighting it.

I untied the cloth, withdrew an inner bundle wrapped in a silk handkerchief, and placed it on the wooden table. Then I quietly unwrapped the silk handkerchief. It fell away to reveal a small lacquer box that glittered bewitchingly in the dim room. A golden frog glistened grotesquely on the lid. Natsume had told me I must not look inside. I slid the black box, still unopened, toward Amagi.

"Open it for me," he said, exhaling a curl of smoke.

"I was told not to look inside." I bowed my head.

Amagi twisted his lips into a smile. His cigarette crackled softly in the dusky room. The smoke smelled awful. A sudden chill ran over me.

Natsume had told me that Amagi was a special customer. I had imagined a pleasantly rotund, good-natured old man, but the aura Amagi exuded was a far cry from that friendly image. I suppose he was around fifty.

"What's your name, then?" he asked, gazing absently at my face. I hesitated for a moment before replying that it was Mutou.

"You hesitated just now. Why?" he asked.

"I did?" I said, feigning innocence. He snorted.

"Never mind. I expect I'll be seeing you again." He grasped the little box that seemed to be lacquered with darkness itself and drew it toward him.

○

Natsume used to live in Tokyo. Back then, her mother was the one who ran Hourendou. I had heard Natsume's father died when she was young. Though her mother continued to run the shop on her own, she eventually fell ill. Natsume, who had already been thinking of returning to Kyoto, left Tokyo to take over the shop. Her mother was admitted to the Red Cross hospital near Tofukuji Temple.

I never met Natsume's mother. Although I didn't know the details of her illness, I gathered from the way Natsume spoke of her that her condition was not good. Usually when I watched the shop, Natsume would take the Keihan Electric Railway to see her at the hospital.

"Tokyo wasn't a good fit for me," she told me once. We had closed up for the night and were sitting across from each other at a low table in the cramped living room behind the shop, eating dinner. Natsume lived back there. She often cooked dinner for me, saying she felt bad that my wages were so low. Given that I lived at a boardinghouse, I was far more grateful for her homemade meals than I would have been to earn a little more per hour. She said she worried that I would waste away from not eating properly, and she cooked all sorts of things for me. In truth, I was skinny because I was lazy, not because I was poor, but I liked being fussed over, and I let myself imagine that she enjoyed fussing over me.

"Now that I've come back to Kyoto, I feel so much calmer. I was always frightened in Tokyo. Everyone else seems to get used to life there, so I thought that in time I would, too, but the fear never went away. My heart was always pounding so hard that it hurt. It really didn't agree with me at all."

She looked down as she spoke, lifting small bites of rice from her bowl into her mouth.

"What were you scared of?" I asked. She smiled as if she didn't know how to answer and fell silent for a few moments. She seemed to be rolling various explanations around in her mouth, carefully selecting the right one.

"Do you ever wake up in the middle of the night all alone and feel afraid for no particular reason?" she finally asked me.

"Yes, sometimes," I replied.

"And then in the morning," she continued, "you have no idea what you were so anxious about. It was like that. In Tokyo, it was always the middle of the night."

○

When I got back from Amagi's mansion, Natsume was bringing in the unglazed water jars and little chests of drawers she always displayed in front of the shop. The sun had long since set, and the light from inside the shop filtered softly through the glass and lit up her face as she bent over her work.

"Amagi is kind of scary, isn't he?" I said as I lent a hand.

"Yes, he is," she mumbled. She had a carved wooden statue of Budai pressed between her small breasts. In her arms, the laughing Buddha looked as soft and fluffy as a kitten. For as long as I'd been working at Hourendou, that old statue had remained unsold. Each morning, Natsume brought him out front into the sun, and each evening she carried him back inside the store in the same manner. This daily ritual of going in and out of the shop seemed to leave them both brimming with satisfaction, and the sight tickled me.

After we finished putting everything away, Natsume turned to me and apologized.

"What for?" I asked.

"I really ought to have gone myself. But I don't like going to that man's house."

"I know what you mean."

"Did Amagi say anything to you?"

"Nothing in particular."

"I see."

Saying no more, she slipped off her shoes and stepped into the back of the shop.

The little lacquer box I'd delivered flashed in my mind. I wondered what could have been inside.

○

I went to Amagi's mansion often. Once I'd experienced what it was like, I began to feel it was my duty to ensure that Natsume never went there again. I suppose I thought of this as repayment for all those dinners she cooked for me.

Most people talk less when they're in a bad mood. Amagi, however, was the opposite. The worse his temper, the more he spoke. I didn't know this at first, and it caught me off guard. I would let myself be lulled into casual conversation, only to be hit with some scathing comment that shocked me back into silence. It angered me, but since he was an important client, I held my tongue.

With time, I grew more cautious and learned to keep my comments to a minimum when he was feeling talkative. But when he was in a truly foul mood, even my silence seemed to fuel his irritation, and there was nothing to be done. In those instances, I focused only on how I might excuse myself.

Our meetings always took place in that bizarrely long, narrow room. Amagi would offer me a cigarette, and the two of us would puff away. He seemed to have an endless supply of them. When winter came and the days grew shorter, he would light paper-covered oil lamps. I never saw him turn on an electric light. The flickering lamplight cast shadows on the darkened *shoji* screens.

Our meetings grew increasingly lengthy, which annoyed me. I would place my bundle on the table only to have him leave it untouched as I grew more and more anxious to depart. Since telling him to hurry up was not an option, I would sit silently on the sofa, waiting. Sometimes a full half hour would pass, broken only by the sound of our cigarettes burning and the bamboo forest rustling outside. It was in these moments that an overblown melancholy would wash over me, and I would feel as if this ghoulish man puffing away before me was consuming my very life itself.

I began to feel certain that Amagi was enjoying all this. I thought how cruel it would be if he had once done the same thing to Natsume that he was now doing to me.

○

"You don't talk much about yourself," said Amagi.

"I'm only the errand boy," I replied.

"Natsume seems to have taken quite a shine to you." He smiled faintly in the light of the lantern. "Since I'm such a recluse, I enjoy the opportunity to talk to someone else now and then. Why don't you open up a little, for my sake?"

"I couldn't do that."

"Why not?"

At a loss for an answer, I took a drag on my cigarette.

"I want to hear more about you. You're in university, aren't you? How do you like it?"

"It's not much fun."

"Your classes bore you?"

"I guess so."

"I was in university for a long time myself. In fact, I was there so long that they finally kicked me out. I remember it as the best time of my life, but in its way, it was also unpleasant. It's hard to pin down, isn't it?"

I listened in silence. I sensed that if I said the wrong thing, I would be dragged into a maze of conversation from which I might never escape. What's more, I found it strange that Amagi would want to hear about other people. He wasn't interested in my idle chatter. I had a vague notion that he was after something else.

"You don't need to be so cautious," he said soothingly. "Everyone's so wary of me; I simply don't understand. How many times have you been here already? Isn't it about time you got used to me? I'm not asking you to bare your soul, of course."

He offered me another cigarette. My tongue was already stinging, and I didn't want to smoke anymore, but I reached for it as a pretext for keeping quiet.

○

After leaving university, Amagi apparently spent a short time working as an instructor at a private high school. However, he quickly quit. I don't know why he became a teacher in the first place. I can't really imagine him standing at a lectern talking to a bunch of scraggly high school kids.

His family owned a fair amount of land in Ichijoji, and there was a storehouse on the grounds full of antiques his father and grandfather had amassed, which could be sold for good money. I assumed

Amagi lived there among the dim shadows by burning through this ancestral wealth.

○

I hadn't made many mistakes in my job at Hourendou, but that day I was out of sorts. My throat had been sore for two days, like I was coming down with a cold, and I'd felt irritable and distracted. Before I knew it, a box had slipped through my fingers. The plate inside tumbled out and cracked badly. It was one of a set I was about to deliver to a client. I could hardly present it to him like this. I had no idea what to do.

Natsume heard the crash and emerged from the back room to come see what had happened.

"I'll pay you back for it," I said gloomily.

"There's no need. But what to do?" She sank into thought, her brow furrowed. "It wasn't particularly valuable, but Sunaga asked for this one specifically, so I can't very well replace it with something else."

"I'll go apologize to him."

She picked up the shards of celadon and placed them back in the box. The gesture reminded me of a bereaved dog owner entombing the bones of their pet. Left with nothing to say, I stared at the nape of her neck as she crouched below me.

"Would you be willing to visit Amagi for me?" she asked.

"Amagi?"

"He'll be able to find something to replace it. I've never told you this, but he's very good at smoothing over difficult situations. We've been going to him for that sort of thing since my parents ran the shop."

"You mean you want me to go to Amagi and ask for something to replace the plate?"

"Yes."

She stood up and peered into my face. A pleasant scent grazed my nose. I thought I felt her tousled bangs brush my forehead. I'd never before looked into her eyes at so close a distance.

"Will you do it?" she asked slowly. "Please tell him I'll repay him in person at a later date. You don't need to do anything else. He may jokingly request something from you, but under no circumstance should you agree. Please do not promise him anything, no matter how insignificant. He's a bit of a peculiar individual."

○

Amagi took out a thick account book and began feverishly writing something down in it. He was wearing old-fashioned round glasses, which made him look like one of those dismal head clerks in a period drama. Maybe his vision had deteriorated from spending all his time in that dusky house.

"Sunaga, you say?"

He went away and came back with an object the size of a soda bottle tied up in cloth.

"Will this be enough?" I asked. He snorted.

"You won't hear any complaints from Sunaga once he sees this. In fact, I expect he'll be quite pleased."

I took the bundle, still only half convinced. Amagi gave me a searching look as he puffed on his cigarette.

"Was there a dispute with Sunaga?" he asked.

"I accidentally broke something I was supposed to deliver to him."

"Natsume must have been furious."

"She never gets angry. But it was inexcusable on my part."

"She's the type who lets it build up. Always has been," Amagi said, as if he'd made sense of the situation. I recalled the gentle way she'd gathered up the broken pieces of pottery.

"She said she'll repay you at a later date."

"Is that so?"

Amagi flipped through his account book. I picked up the bundle, planning to thank him and leave. He shut the book with a clap.

"I've got a favor to ask," he said, gazing at the eerie pictures on the sliding doors around us, now illuminated in the afternoon sun. "A little something in return for what I've done, eh?"

I recalled what Natsume had said to me, her face so close that our foreheads were almost touching. *Please do not promise him anything, no matter how insignificant. He's a bit of a peculiar individual.*

"You bear some responsibility, after all."

"I do, but..."

"Did she say something to you? Something about not giving me anything?"

"No, of course not."

Amagi smiled.

"It's a simple request. Does your room have a kerosene heater?"

"No, it's electric."

"That's what I want."

○

Sunaga was apparently extremely satisfied with the object Amagi had given me. In fact, he bought several other items that had been sitting around Hourendou unsold. Amagi's mysterious certainty had turned out to be entirely correct.

Two days after my visit, I brought him my electric heater. It was an old thing I'd been using since I started university, so I didn't mind parting with it. The weather wasn't too cold yet, and if it got to be unbearable, I could just buy a new one. I had no idea why Amagi would want such a thing.

However, since Natsume had been so insistent about not giving him anything, I didn't tell her what I'd done. For her part, she never brought up the incident again.

○

When Naoko heard I was working at Hourendou, she stopped by.

We'd been dating for a year and a half. Since I spent my weekends at Hourendou and we were both busy with school during the week, we didn't go out often. A week or so earlier, we'd gone out for the first time in a while to see the fall leaves at Kiyomizu-dera and gotten into a stupid argument. I wouldn't give in, and neither would she, so we parted on bad terms. I hadn't heard from her since. I'd been looking for a chance to patch things up, so I was happy to see her walk into Hourendou.

Natsume was resting upstairs with a cold, and I was watching the store by myself. Sitting with a printout of an academic paper in one hand and a dictionary in the other, I heard the clatter of the glass door. When I looked up, Naoko was standing there with an awkward expression on her face.

Naoko was in the same year as me, and we were majoring in the same subject. She was short and came off as cute at first glance, but when she got pissed off, she would mercilessly turn her scathing tongue on just about anything.

She sat in a chair sipping a cup of green tea and looking around, her eyes sparkling.

"Neat place," she said. "Is everything expensive?"

"Some of it is, but not as bad as you'd think. This isn't a high-end shop."

"So are you an expert on antiques now?"

"Nah, I just watch the shop and deliver stuff. I don't know anything."

Suddenly Naoko glanced toward the back and bowed her head. I turned around to find Natsume standing in a daze, a shawl around her shoulders. She looked like she still had a fever.

"Welcome," she said.

When I introduced Naoko to her, she said, "I've heard a lot about you."

It was only three, and there was still plenty of time before evening, but she suggested that we close the shop early. I asked Naoko to wait while I helped Natsume close up. Her breathing was labored, which worried me.

"I'm fine," she said. "We'll take the day off tomorrow. Please come back next Saturday."

○

Naoko had been in a good mood when she was surrounded by old curios, but over dinner she was withdrawn, and all my attempts at conversation ran up against a stone wall. She was always like that when she had something to say that she was keeping inside.

The stone wall showed no sign of crumbling even when we got back to my room.

"You still haven't taken out your heater?" she asked out of nowhere.

"It broke," I lied. She was silent for a few moments, and so was I.

"She seems like a lonely person."

At first I didn't know who she was talking about, but then I realized she meant Natsume. I thought of her standing unsteadily at the back of the shop with that feverish look in her eyes.

"Yeah."

"I got a little shiver when she came out of the back like that."

"Why?"

"She looked like a ghost or something."

"Probably because she was sick. She said she was running a thirty-eight-degree fever."

"Maybe." She glanced absently at my bookshelf. "I'm freezing," she muttered.

In place of the heater, I pulled out my futon.

After we'd been under the covers for a while, the comforter took on some of our body heat and softened up. I pressed my face against hers. She looked up at me through her bangs. I brushed my lips against her cold cheeks and breathed in her scent. The wall of grumpiness had finally crumbled.

"It's getting colder, so you'd better buy a heater," she said. "You'll get sick if you don't."

○

In December, the cold became more intense. As long as I spent most of the day in lecture halls and labs and immediately dove into my futon when I got back home, I could get by all right without a heater. Mornings were tough, though. It was miserable to get dressed while shivering in a room that had been losing heat all night.

I hadn't crossed the threshold of Amagi's mansion for about two weeks. I didn't have any errands there, and he didn't contact the shop, either.

Business was slow at Hourendou, and the already sparse stream of customers grew thinner still. I spent my time there writing up lab results and talking with Natsume.

She brought an old heater out of the storeroom and set it next to the counter. It made the shop even cozier.

Sometimes Natsume bought sake lees from a brewery in the neighborhood and toasted them over the heater. She didn't drink, but she liked to eat the lees piled with sugar. When she did, her cheeks would flush, and she would act like a giggly little girl. I know it's strange to compare a thirtysomething woman taller than me to a little girl, but I couldn't shake the image.

Naoko visited now and then, and the three of us would chat together. At first, Natsume was quiet in front of Naoko, but she gradually warmed up and even invited her to dinner a few times.

"She's a sweet girl," Natsume told me. Hearing that made Naoko happy.

I thought the year would end peacefully just like that.

But then Amagi called, and I went to his house again.

○

When I walked into Amagi's garden, he was sitting on the veranda. A large, upturned basket was next to him, and he was peering inside through the slats.

When he noticed me, he smiled and said, "Ah, there you are."

"What's that?" I asked.

"I received a strange creature from an acquaintance of mine."

As I got close to the basket, the smell of wet dog hit my nose. The inside was dark, so I couldn't tell what was lurking within. Listening closely, I made out a faint whimpering and sensed something moving restlessly about inside. I bent over next to Amagi and peered in. For a brief instant, I thought I glimpsed a pair of human eyes staring back at me.

Shocked, I looked up. Amagi was yawning like he was bored.

"Whatever will I do about this?" he said. "Anyway, come inside."

After we moved to the usual room and I handed him the package from Natsume, I lit the cigarette he offered me.

The room was bitingly cold and the freezing leather of the sofa intolerable. The small gray hibachi that had been set next to it was no match for the chill. Nevertheless, Amagi was wearing the same bright blue kimono as always, his thin chest showing where the fabric crossed. Just looking at him made me feel ill. I wondered if he had dressed like that purely to harass me, then told myself I was overthinking the situation. I got the feeling, too, that he could see each of these thoughts play out in my mind.

"Your room must be cold without a heater," he said in a kindly voice.

"It's fine."

"It's going to get much colder, you know."

"I suppose."

"It's not all bad, though. If a girl comes to your room, you'll have an excuse to cuddle up, eh?"

"Maybe."

"A nice young man like you must have a girlfriend."

"No, I'm not into all that."

"Are you sure?"

"Yes."

"Winter's a fine thing if you've got someone to snuggle up against. Warm each other up under the blankets, if you know what I mean."

"Come on."

I smiled wryly and looked away, tracing the frame of a *shoji* screen with my eyes. The way he talked, as if he'd been there watching us, was uncanny. I tried to act like the suggestion was absurd, but I felt like a lump of mud had been dropped into the bottom of my stomach.

"Did I make you angry?" he asked with a smile. "You probably hate this kind of talk."

I thought I saw a shadow appear on the screen facing the courtyard. But the day was overcast, so perhaps a stray cloud had only skimmed across the sun.

"Is someone in the garden?" I asked. Amagi's expression suddenly tensed, the skin tightening across his face. His eyes stopped moving, as if they'd frozen solid inside their deep sockets.

"In the garden? Who?" he asked sharply, his eyes still fixed on my face.

"Oh, no, I just thought I saw something."

Slowly, he craned his neck around to gaze at the screen. He sniffed the air for a moment, then let out a relieved sigh.

"Not a soul."

"Of course. I must have imagined it."

Amagi smiled self-deprecatingly and sank back into the sofa.

"So you don't have anyone to warm you up, eh? Poor boy. Shall I give back your heater, then?"

"I'd be grateful if you did."

"I happen to be searching for something at the moment. If you find it for me, I'll return the heater. What do you say?"

As I wrestled with what I should say in response, he spread out his bony fingers and covered his face with both hands, as if breaking down in tears. His face darkened beneath his palms, and his eyes peered out from between his fingers. I stared at him in surprise.

"I'm looking for a fox mask," he said.

I had heard that Sunaga lived in the Kitashirakawa district, where he had long owned land. Many of the apartments and rental properties nearby belonged to him, and he had been frequenting Hourendou since Natsume's parents ran it. Natsume told me that after her father died, it was Sunaga who moved the shop to Ichijoji and made sure her mother was able to continue the business. Although I felt beholden to him for breaking the plate I was supposed to deliver, I had never met the man. Natsume told me he was over seventy but very energetic for his age.

One Sunday morning near the end of December, I arrived at Hourendou to find her talking to an older man. He had a round belly and a cheerful expression exactly like the statue of Budai that she carried in and out of the shop every day. His mood was clearly infectious, because Natsume was smiling as happily as a cat lolling in the sun. I immediately guessed he must be Sunaga. He was wearing a stylish coat and had a brown hat in his hand.

"Good morning," I called out.

"This is the young man I was just telling you about," Natsume said, still smiling.

"Ah, I see. The young man who broke my plate?"

He laughed loudly, and I flushed.

I went to the back of the shop to use the bathroom, and as I returned, I overheard the two of them still talking.

"Honestly, though, Natsume, you must watch out for Amagi."

"I know."

"I'd be lying if I said I wasn't happy to receive it, but you really don't need to do that anymore."

"I'm sorry."

"I'm not scolding you. You have nothing to apologize for." Sunaga coughed. "Anyway, be careful."

"I will. Thank you."

That day, Sunaga sat in the shop for a long time, sipping tea, laughing, and eating the selection of cakes he'd brought with him. From what he said, it seemed his family doctor had forbidden him from eating sweets, and he wasn't allowed to eat them at home, so he ate them in secret when he went out. Taking this opportunity to do just that, the old man crammed cake after cake into his mouth, puffing in between on a sweet-smelling cigar.

"You won't tell on me, will you, Natsume?" he pleaded.

"No, but please don't overdo it," she answered. "I'd be very sad if you died from eating too many cakes at my shop."

"I'm not going to die!"

He roared with laughter, then theatrically stabbed another cake and devoured it. I felt I could understand why his doctor had forbidden them.

* * *

As Sunaga was leaving, he withdrew a wooden box from a paper bag he had set on the floor and held it out to Natsume.

"This is for you."

Natsume let out a gasp of delight as she opened it.

At first glance, it looked like a simple black lacquer tray. But off in one corner was a single bright red Ranchu goldfish. The round little fish looked as if it might flap its delicate fins at any moment. As I gazed at the tray, the flat black lacquer began to resemble the glistening surface of a bottomless pool.

"Oh!" Natsume exclaimed, pointing at the goldfish. "I think it just moved!"

"It does move," Sunaga announced proudly. I wasn't sure if he was joking or being serious.

"I can't accept something like this." Natsume shook her head even as she continued to stare at the tray, bewitched.

"Isn't today the day you were born?" Sunaga said, like he was explaining something to a child.

"Dear me," Natsume answered, glancing blankly off into space.

○

After Sunaga left, Natsume began cleaning the storeroom.

It was full of things that had been there since her parents ran the shop that she couldn't sell and didn't know what to do with. She said she planned to get rid of them before the year's end. She told me I could take anything I wanted, but nothing she brought out was even remotely appealing to me. There were even some tubes for a centrifuge. I had never dreamed I'd see lab equipment at Hourendou.

As she was working, Natsume suddenly let out a yelp, so I peered into the storeroom after her. A papier-mâché fox mask wrapped in yellowed newspaper was lying on the ground.

"Completely caught me by surprise," Natsume said. "I don't much care for that."

"Then do you mind if I take it?"

"Not at all."

I picked up the old mask and turned it over in my hands. It was much lighter than I'd expected and completely ordinary in every respect.

"Do you not like foxes?" I asked.

"That mask reminds me of Fushimi Inari Shrine. Don't you think that's a creepy place?"

"You're right—it is a little scary. I've been there before."

"Once, a long time ago, I went there with my mother," she said.

"We went to worship Inari, the god of foxes. I can't remember why or why it was only the two of us. I was still quite young. My mother pulled me by the hand through that long, seemingly endless tunnel of *torii* gates, deeper and deeper into the woods. That fox mask was dangling from her hand. I think someone had forgotten it at the teahouse on the mountain pass where we stopped to rest, and she took it. It was the hottest part of summer, but for some reason when we entered Inari's forest, the air was so cool, I felt my whole body go damp, and I remember shivers running constantly down the back of my neck. No matter how far we went, there were always more rows of old moss-covered lanterns and statues of the foxes that serve as Inari's messengers. The heavy smell of burning candles seemed to penetrate my body, making me feel sick. I was so frightened, but the scariest thing of all—"

Natsume stared at the fox mask in my hands.

"—was my mother's face. She was walking half a pace ahead of me, so I was looking up at her face from behind at an angle, and she had such an eerie expression, like nothing I'd ever seen before. Like she was angry, or laughing, or crying. No matter how many times I looked up at her, I couldn't make out which it was. But I knew with a horrible certainty that it was not my mother's ordinary face. I even wondered if this was not my mother at all but instead some creature that had taken her place and planned to spirit me away into the depths of Inari's forest. She swung the fox mask in her right hand and held my hand with her left. But her long, slack fingers had no strength in them. But what if she turned around the instant I let go, staring back at me from the stone steps with a face that really was not her own, but something else entirely? Such a mistake could never be undone. That thought was what kept me walking on, my hand in hers."

She laughed dryly, as if even now she was still trying to shake off this thing that had been clinging to her shoulders from childhood.

"Children are odd, you know. They imagine things like that, frightening themselves more and more. And then they remember them clear as day forever after. But I wonder, if I'd given in to the fear that day and shaken off my mother's hand to run away, what *would* her face have looked like when she turned around? I still think about it sometimes."

She hugged her thin frame with both arms and stared again at the mask in my hands. The fox face stared back at her, its enigmatic expression frozen in place.

○

The next day, Natsume went to the Red Cross hospital while I watched the shop.

I was sitting with my elbows on the counter, dozing off. The hot air from the heater was making my cheeks tingle. I hadn't been able to fall asleep until late the previous night, and I felt ill, as if a fog were hanging between my eyes.

Although it wasn't yet two, the sky outside the glass doors was dark as dusk, and the air had a reddish-gray cast to it. The clouds must have been to blame. Every time I jerked awake, the scene outside was darker. My right cheek was covered in sweat where I was propping it up with the palm of my hand. I would think about turning down the heater, then doze off again before I managed to stand up. That cycle seemed to repeat itself endlessly.

I wondered if Natsume was ever coming back.

Between sleep and wakefulness, my mood worsened. Images flitted across my mind of Natsume yelping like she'd been stung by an insect when she discovered the fox mask, of myself walking through the gate to Amagi's mansion, and of Amagi sitting on the sofa at the end of that strangely long room, the fox mask covering his face. Maybe the reason my right cheek was sweating was because those unpleasant memories had wormed their way into my dreams.

As I succumbed to this uncomfortable sleep, I began to wonder if I shouldn't have given Amagi the mask. I hadn't intended to go along with his bargain in the first place. I'd had no attachment to that heater. Rather than entangle myself further with Amagi, I'd have much rather bought a new heater. The fox mask just happened to show up at my feet, and I made the mistake of giving it to him.

Actually, even when I'd gone to his house the previous evening on an errand, I hadn't intended to give it to him. I'd kept it shut away in my bag, but he'd sensed it, and I couldn't lie my way out of the situation.

"So you found it," he'd said. A paper bag containing my heater was already sitting in a corner of the room. Had he somehow known I would find a fox mask that day?

He'd picked up the mask and fit it over his face. Then he'd fallen silent.

For some time, the fox man and I had faced each other across that dark room.

Finally, I shook off my sleepiness enough to stand up and turn down the heater. Then I walked over to the glass door looking out on the street and pressed my hot forehead against the pane, which was cool from the outside air. The afternoon had grown even darker.

Alone there in the quiet of Hourendou with a gloomy sky outside, I felt vaguely uneasy, as if some uncanny presence was there with me in the room. Every time I looked at the hibachis and Japanese wardrobes gathering dust in the corner, I remembered Amagi. I didn't know how he'd managed to sink his claws so deeply into my soul.

I stretched my arms over my head, hoping to shake off the uneasiness, then turned around. A man was standing between the shop and the back room, looking at me. He was wearing a fox mask. Goose bumps rose across the skin of my sides and back. Behind the fox mask, the man made a sound like phlegm was caught in his throat.

Just as I was about to leap up, I heard what sounded like a crowd of people throwing pebbles at the shop's glass door. It was raining. All the moisture that had been building up in the atmosphere seemed to gush from the sky at once in a furious downpour. I glanced over my shoulder. The scene outside the window had vanished as if it were covered in smoke.

When I looked toward the back of the shop again, the man was gone.

I stood, unmoving, until Natsume returned.

Natsume entered the shop, brushing drops of water from her shoulders.

"What's the matter? You're white as a sheet."

"There was a person back there."

"A person?"

Natsume quickly pulled off her shoes and walked toward the back of the shop. She set her handbag on the low table in the living room, and I could hear her pattering around. She returned with a suspicious look on her face. "There's no one back there," she said.

"He was wearing a fox mask."

"Why would you say something so frightening?" she asked, sounding suddenly angry.

She stared at me. I could see the blood drain from her face. Watching her, I realized I was having the same reaction.

Natsume didn't say much as she closed up the shop that night. She looked as if she'd drunk poison. Once the rain stopped, I felt as if I'd woken from a bad dream and was sorry for scaring her with my sleep-addled nonsense.

She asked me to stay for dinner, and I agreed because she didn't seem herself. I was supposed to meet with Naoko, but I called her and apologized. Since explaining the situation would have been difficult, I lied and said a friend from high school had shown up unexpectedly.

Natsume and I sat down at the table, but she hardly touched her food.

"You should eat a little more," I said.

"I'm fine. I never eat much."

The weak glow of the fluorescent bulb didn't reach her downturned face. "That light needs to be changed," I said, then continued eating in silence. Across the table, her features seemed to gradually harden into white stone. Seeing her sit there like a lifeless doll, I felt my chest tighten. I couldn't swallow the rest of my rice, so I poured some tea over it and slurped it down without chewing.

"I know it's wrong to ask this of you," she said, looking down again. "But would you mind staying the night?"

"I'm sorry," I said, shaking my head. "I can't."

"Yes, of course not." She nodded.

Her gaze dropped to the tatami mat below her, then darted to the darkened shop and behind her to the stairs leading to the second floor. Each time she looked searchingly into the darkness, I wished she wouldn't. The more she did, the more certain I was she'd find something crouching there in the shadows.

"I'll sleep upstairs, and you can sleep down here. That would be enough."

She bowed her head deeply.

○

I stared at the light bulb hanging above. Wrapped in a coarse, unfamiliar *yukata*, staring up at an unfamiliar ceiling, I remembered staying at my grandparents' house in the countryside as a child. I had trouble falling asleep, so I used to shake my grandmother, who always drifted off before me, until she woke. Then she would stay up until I fell asleep. Just knowing someone else was awake was enough to soothe me.

I glanced at the clock. It was just past two in the morning. Time seemed to be passing both slowly and quickly, and I felt disoriented. Perhaps I had drifted off a few times without realizing it.

Suddenly, I sensed someone nearby and sat up. A figure was standing in the shadows at the base of the stairs to the second floor. I almost cried out before realizing it was Natsume, come down from upstairs. She was wearing white pajamas with a wool shawl around her shoulders.

"I'm sorry—did I wake you?" she whispered.

"No, I couldn't sleep."

"Neither could I."

Stepping apologetically across my feet, she walked to the kitchen and set a kettle on the stove. I gazed at her back from where I sat in my futon. In the dusky orange shadows, her figure floated faintly, like a phantom. A wave of drowsiness overtook me as I listened to the soft clattering of kitchen utensils.

"Would you like a cup of tea?" she asked, turning toward me. The gesture struck me as incredibly alluring.

We sat on the tatami mat, drinking tea. She smiled, a hint of fear in her expression.

"I didn't tell you yesterday," she said, "but I have another horribly frightening memory related to fox masks."

"It happened when I was in elementary school. At the time, we lived in the Jodoji district. My family already ran a shop called Hourendou, although in a different location. I loved the New Year's holiday, but in February it was Setsubun that I looked forward to. Yoshida Shrine holds a grand festival for the occasion, with hordes of people and night stalls as far as the eye can see. It takes place in the coldest part of February, and it often snowed. The festival was always lovely in the snow. I'll never forget the feeling of climbing the hill to the shrine as the snow crunched under my feet and slipping into the lively festival crowd.

"From this side of Yoshida Hill, you could hardly even tell there was a festival. But as you got closer, the stinging, cold air gradually warmed, and at a certain point, everything suddenly became bright, like a light had been switched on. The faces of the people walking down the path looked so delightfully warm and flushed, you'd never have guessed it was winter. Walking among them, caught up in the mood of the festival, my body would become light, and I would begin to feel that even if I didn't move my feet, the crowd would carry me along endlessly.

"On that day, too, I must have been floating along with that same drunken sensation. I'd already crossed onto the shrine grounds and descended the stone stairs, and I was walking down the long path leading to the shrine amid the river of people.

"A tall man was walking next to me, wearing a fox mask. Because we were at a festival, I didn't find it strange.

"After we had walked along like that for a little while, the man suddenly turned his face toward me. I'm not sure what it was, but he made a strange, frightening sound like phlegm was caught in his throat, then twisted his neck to look up at the sky. He seemed to be in great pain, but since he was wearing the fox mask, it felt like he was only playacting. Then, with his head still twisted, he collapsed onto his back. Shocked, I stood stock-still and stared at him as he lay on the ground.

"He was twitching bizarrely. He seemed to be in anguish, as if, still alive, he could feel his body was being twisted apart. But the mask he had put on in jest clung to his face and couldn't be removed."

Natsume sighed and took a sip of tea.

"What happened to him?" I asked.

"He died," she answered. "I haven't been to the Setsubun Festival since."

I didn't sleep for the rest of the night. I had Natsume bring a desk lamp down from upstairs, and I sat at the low table reading a textbook. Knowing that I was awake seemed to calm her, and after sitting on my futon and chatting for a while, she eventually fell asleep there.

○

On weekdays, I spent my time either at the university or in my room, and on weekends I was buried among the curios of Hourendou, so I hardly even noticed Christmas approaching. When I went to Sanjo for a year-end party with some classmates, I found the city sparkling with decorations that had gone up while I wasn't looking. The twenty-fifth was just around the corner.

Naoko and I were both the type to ignore things the more those around us got worked up, but we did have a decent feast in her room on Christmas. She gave me a book of paintings I'd been wanting, and I gave her a little coral broach I'd bought at Hourendou.

We were hanging out in her room when, around nine in the evening, Natsume called me. This was unusual.

"I'm sorry to make such an unreasonable request, but I'd like you to return that mask."

She seemed to be calling from outside somewhere. I pictured her shielding the phone from the noise of the street as she spoke with difficulty.

"You mean the fox mask?" I asked, realizing I was in trouble. The mask was already in Amagi's hands. When I hesitated, Natsume continued. "When I told her I'd given it away, she was furious. She keeps saying it's hers and that I must get it back. There's no persuading her."

"You're sure there's no other way?" I asked.

She apologized several times. She seemed to be bowing her head on the other end of the line. "I know it's selfish of me to ask after the fact, but this illness has made my mother so temperamental. I simply don't know what to do."

"All right, I understand. I'll bring it to you soon."

"I'm sorry. I appreciate it," Natsume said. She sounded on the verge of tears.

After I hung up, I sank into thought.

I could hardly imagine Amagi giving the mask back of his own free will. Since it was the kind of papier-mâché trinket you could find anywhere, I thought maybe I could fool her by giving her a similar one. But could I?

"What's the matter?" Naoko asked, peering worriedly into my face.

○

The following evening, I paid a visit to Amagi's mansion.

When I stood before the open veranda and called out a greeting, he emerged with Sunaga by his side.

"Hello there!" Sunaga called out. Although he smiled at me, he looked horribly haggard standing there in that dark room. His cheeks were slick with sweat. I remember thinking how strange that was on such a piercingly cold evening.

Sunaga was apparently about to leave, and he stepped down into the garden as I stepped toward the house. He looked so shaky on his feet, I instinctively reached out a hand to steady him. "Sorry," he said. Amagi stood on the veranda with his arms crossed, smiling faintly.

"Please don't mention that I was here," he said, struggling for breath as he put on his shoes. "To Natsume, I mean."

I nodded.

Amagi looked at me and snorted a laugh. "Come," he said.

I slipped off my shoes and stepped up to the veranda, watching Sunaga stumble out of the garden. He looked so unwell, I wanted to run over and shake him. Not a trace remained of the warmth he had exuded the day he sat in Hourendou gobbling down cakes.

Eventually, the sound of his uneven footsteps faded, leaving only the rustling of the bamboo grove.

When I pleaded, head bowed, for Amagi to return the fox mask, he told me to show him my wallet. I had no idea what he was after. I said I didn't want to.

"All you have to do is show me," he said. The fox mask was sitting on the table.

I held out my wallet, and Amagi took it, looking pleased. He flipped it around in his fingers, so slender that they looked like bare bone. He seemed to be getting skinnier and skinnier. Nevertheless, he was wearing that dingy blue kimono, the same as the day I met him.

Presently, he pulled from the wallet a small, cutout photograph of Naoko.

"I'll take this."

"You can't."

I reached for it, but he swiftly stuck it in his mouth and held up his hands, bent like hawk talons, to fend me off. His thin lips glinted crimson in the darkness.

○

New Year's had passed and university classes were just beginning when Natsume's mother died at the Red Cross hospital.

Once she got through the initial fluster of activity following the death, Natsume stayed cooped up at the back of her dim rooms, squeezing her body into a stiff ball. Hourendou grew as dark as if it had sunk to the bottom of a lake, and behind a sign reading CLOSED FOR THE DAY, the glass door remained shut. Even on those sunny, bracing days when it felt good to be outside despite the cold, the smile of the wooden Budai statue was absent from the shop front.

I finally saw her again around the middle of January.

"I don't think my mother had any regrets," she said. Her face seemed frozen solid as she set fire to the fox mask on the street in front of Hourendou. Her mother had died gripping it in her hands.

I tried to imagine the face of this woman I had never once met. She was wearing the fox mask as she lay on her deathbed. She writhed like the masked man Natsume had watched die when she was a child. She was in anguish, like she could feel her body being twisted apart while she was still alive, but the mask she had put on in jest clung to her face and couldn't be removed.

○

As time passed, I became increasingly uncomfortable.

I started to feel as if giving Amagi the photograph of Naoko had been a truly irreparable mistake.

I met with Naoko as often as I could. I felt that if I lost sight of her, a set of talons would reach out from that dark mansion to grab her and drag her back into the murky twilight.

○

"Fox tales," Naoko said. We were in my room.

I looked up from the sake lees I had been toasting on the stove and glanced over my shoulder at her in surprise. She was sitting on the tatami with her arms wrapped around her knees, staring up absently at the ceiling. With her hair cut short again, she looked as clean and fresh as a young boy.

"What?" I asked.

She started telling me about the country town where she'd grown up.

Foxes lived in the forest there, and they often bewitched people. Long ago, when her grandparents were young, fox mischief was common. They would turn themselves into beautiful women, or gather in long, mysterious processions, or steal the souvenirs off her grandfather as he walked, slightly tipsy, leaving only the wrapping cloth behind. Naoko smiled as she told me these stories.

"I'm sure foxes don't do those things anymore," I said.

"No, they do," she said, shaking her head. "Once when I was in grade school, I saw a fox fire. I don't remember why, but I was walking along the paths between the rice paddies with a flashlight, and across the fields was a long stretch of pitch-black hills. In the dark forest at the base of the hills, I saw a blinking light. But as soon as I noticed it twinkling, the light whizzed through the air into another patch of forest. That was a fox fire."

"You're kidding."

"No, it's true."

She glared at me playfully.

I sprinkled sugar over the sake lees and arranged the pieces on a plate. "So these are sake lees!" Naoko said happily, cutting them into slivers and putting one into her mouth.

I lit a cigarette. "Why did you bring that up all of a sudden?" I asked.

Chewing enthusiastically, she said, "I'm not sure," then sank into thought. Finally, a glint came into her eye. "I remember now! You know those fox masks?"

"You mean the ones they sell at festival stalls?"

"Yeah, the papier-mâché ones kids wear." She gently covered her face with one hand. Her eyes stared out from between her fingers. "I saw a man with one on his face. Let's see… I think it was on the way to school the other day. Weird, huh?"

I walked her back to her apartment.

"You don't have to. It's not even that far," she said.

"From now on, I wish you wouldn't go out walking at night," I said. She gave me a suspicious look.

As we walked down the darkened street, we passed fluorescent streetlamps at regular intervals that cast a white glow on the sidewalk. Ahead of us, one was on the verge of burning out, its light blinking in the night. It would dim and flicker, but just when I thought it would go out, it would snap back on, as if changing its mind, then begin to dim and flicker again, like it was mocking us. I felt like I was watching someone sway perilously as they nodded off on a train.

"I hate that," Naoko whispered. "I wish they'd replace it already."

As I stared into the shadows beneath the broken light, I thought I could make out a figure standing there just as it went dark. But when the light came on again, no one was there.

"Oh?" Naoko said, gripping my coat.

The light went out with a snap. In that instant, I thought I saw a shadowy human figure twisting beneath it.

○

The next time I went to Hourendou, Natsume was dressed in mourning attire. She was shivering faintly, her delicate hands clasped over her chest. Mourning clothes aren't cheerful to start with, but on her, the effect was unbearably pitiful.

"I have to go out. Please watch the shop for me," she said, carrying the Budai statue out into the sun.

"Did somebody die?" I asked.

"Sunaga passed away." Her lips twisted as if she were laughing and crying at the same time. Wrapped in her arms, the Budai statue seemed to be roaring with laughter like Sunaga had on the day he ate cakes at Hourendou.

"Are you all right?" I asked.

"Yes, I'm fine. I just never expected Sunaga to pass this soon," she said.

Her arms still wrapped around the statue, she began to weep.

Later, I learned that Sunaga had met a strange end.

On the day of his death, members of his household had begun, under his direction, to clean out the storehouse on his property. He was the sort of person who insisted on doing things as soon as they occurred to him, so everyone thought it was just another of his whims. But while he was normally satisfied once a bit of work had been done, this time he seemed bent on thoroughly reorganizing the storehouse. He even lugged things around himself until he was covered in dust, refusing to let anyone stop him. They thought perhaps he was searching for something.

In the afternoon, saying he deserved a treat because he'd worked so hard, Sunaga sent for some cakes and ate them with relish. When the others tried to rein him in, he ignored them, cackling with laughter and saying, "Oh, it doesn't matter anymore." Then he gave an energetic cheer and went back to work.

Since the job was far too large to finish in one day, they used tarps to cover all the old things they'd hauled into the garden, leaving the rest of the work for the next day. But even after the others had gone inside, Sunaga stayed out in the storehouse pacing about.

Worried when he did not return even as dusk fell and the cold grew bitter, someone went out to the storehouse to check on him. They found him hanging inside. His wet cheeks glistened in the ray of evening light that lanced through the open doors.

He left no suicide note.

○

A memory flickered across my mind of Sunaga the day I'd run into him in Amagi's garden. He had looked so haggard, almost as if he'd shrunk a size. I'd felt as though a death spirit were clinging to his back.

I imagined Sunaga and Amagi in that long, dim room, trading antiques. Sunaga had asked me not to tell Natsume he was there. What had he received from Amagi? And what had he given in return?

I wondered if, perhaps, Sunaga had been lured into his dealings with Amagi by the contents of that cloth-wrapped bundle I'd given him in exchange for the broken plate. If that was true, it meant Amagi had used me as his cat's paw. I shivered.

An image of Sunaga, ensnared by Amagi and unable to move, overlapped in my mind with a vision of his body hanging in the storehouse. As he swung back and forth, he begged me not to tell Natsume his secret, voice thick with tears. Then the image morphed into the man who had died wearing the fox mask, then into Natsume's mother, then Natsume, myself, and finally Amagi.

A bored smile turned up the corners of Amagi's lips as he swung back and forth.

○

Although spring was still a long way off and the cold was worse than ever, I tried my best to act cheerful and keep my gloomy memories in check around Natsume. But in a corner of my heart lurked an eerie, undeniable awareness that I was still in the middle of my transaction with Amagi. I felt as if a fist-size lump of lead lay at the bottom of my stomach.

After finishing work one evening, I was getting ready to go

home when Natsume mumbled, "Amagi called to say he needs something."

"Are you going?" I asked.

"No, not me," she answered apologetically. "It's you he wants to see."

I felt the lump of lead swell as I stood in a daze, gripping my bag.

"Um, it sounds like he has some sort of present for Naoko."

"For Naoko?"

Natsume peered at me, a worried look on her face.

○

"I see, so she burned the mask."

Amagi laughed. We were in the same room as always, and as always, it was dark. A cigarette in hand, Amagi launched into a story. "I had a particular attachment to that mask, you see."

"It happened long ago, just around this time of year. I may be a recluse, but sometimes I do go out, and since the Setsubun Festival at Yoshida Shrine is quite a grand event, I make a point of going every year. Once, I was walking from Higashioji Street down the path leading to the main shrine. It snowed that year on Setsubun, and the sight of the long rows of night stalls all lit up as the snow fell silently over them was terribly charming. The grounds were packed with people, and their faces all looked so warm and comfortable.

"I don't remember exactly what I ate, but I'd bought a skewer of grilled chicken or something and was eating it as I walked along. Threading my way through the crowd, I saw a strange pair coming toward me. One was a young girl and the other a grown man. The man was wearing a fox mask, which wasn't so unnatural in the lively air of the festival. He just seemed to be having a good time.

"But as they drew near me, something changed. The man suddenly began to act strangely. He looked down at the little girl next to him. Then, I'm not sure what happened, but he made a strange, frightening sound like phlegm was caught in his throat, and he twisted his neck to look up at the sky. He seemed to be in great pain, but since he was wearing the fox mask, it felt like he was only playacting. Then, with his head still twisted, he collapsed onto his back.

"I stood stock-still, staring at him. He was twitching. He seemed to be in anguish, as if, still alive, he could feel his body was being twisted apart. But the mask he had put on in jest clung to his face and couldn't be removed.

"Eventually, a middle-aged man came running to his side and pulled him into a sitting position. He tore off the fox mask, but foam was spilling from the fallen man's mouth, and his face was horribly distorted. He was already dead. When I saw him without the mask, I finally realized he was the owner of Hourendou, who I knew through business. The man who had come to his aid yelled for someone to call a doctor, but I knew it was already too late.

"The girl stood still as a statue. 'Natsume, Natsume!' the middle-aged man shouted, but she didn't answer. She must have been in shock. I bought a candy apple from one of the stalls and gave it to her. In return, she handed me the bag of puffed rice she had been holding. 'You're Natsume?' I asked, but she just stood there, silently gripping the stick of the candy apple.

"The man holding the corpse looked at me.

"'What a terrible thing, Sunaga,' I said to him."

* * *

Amagi watched me through the smoke like he was studying my reaction, but I remained silent.

"If that's all you have to say, I'll be going now, since it's getting late," I said.

"That it is, but I'd hoped you'd stay for dinner," he answered, looking up at the clock on the wall.

"No, I can't. I've got to get going now."

"What a pity that would be, since I made it just for you. Wait here for a minute, won't you? I'll run and get it."

He stood, slid open the painted screen, and left the room. I'd never seen what was on the other side, but since he opened it just a crack to slip through, I couldn't catch a glimpse.

With Amagi gone, silence settled around me. The courtyard beyond the *shoji* was completely dark by now, and the screens reflected the flickering light of candles. I thought about leaving without a word, but as I hesitated, Amagi returned. Although he'd promised me dinner, there was only a single red bowl on the black lacquer tray he carried.

"It's not much, but..."

"No, that's plenty."

"Well, take off the lid and have a sip."

I lifted the tightly fitted lid. A curl of white steam wafted up with a delicious aroma. A dark-green piece of something, maybe wakame, was swaying in the translucent soup. Steeling my will, I took a sip. The soft, slippery substance seemed to tangle around my tongue for the longest time. It tasted sweet and sour.

"Tasty, eh?" Amagi said smugly, bringing a bowl to his own lips. "The bowl is special, too."

I wanted to drink it down as quickly as possible so I could

go home, but I seemed to be making little progress on the hot, slippery soup. When I had finally managed to finish a little more than half, I realized a green frog was sitting at the bottom of the quivering liquid, and I nearly vomited.

"Oh, don't worry about that. It's only a picture," Amagi said nonchalantly.

As he'd said, there was an intricate drawing at the bottom of the black bowl, but the picture didn't show only a frog. As I drank more of the soup, and more of the image came into view, I felt as if Amagi were gripping my heart with his bare hands. My mind went blank as I was overcome with a fury so great, it frightened even me.

The drawing at the bottom of the bowl was of Naoko. Her plump, naked body was on all fours, her face turned down. Her short hair was disheveled, as if it was swaying in the water. A large frog sat heavily on her naked back.

I flipped the bowl over, flinging out the rest of the soup.

"Didn't you like the taste?" Amagi asked with a smile. "There's something else I'd like to show you. A magic lantern I made myself. It's quite unique."

"I'll be going now," I said, standing up. "And I won't be back."

As I walked swiftly down the hallway, I heard Amagi call out, "Oh, you'll be back."

○

I tried to see Naoko that night, but I couldn't reach her. I called her over and over, every few minutes, but she didn't answer.

The next day, I stopped by her apartment but saw no sign of her inside. When I asked her friends at school, no one knew anything.

My anxiety ballooned. I stumbled through the city, searching anywhere I thought she might go, but I didn't find her.

When I asked her landlord for help, he called her parents for me, but she hadn't gone home. To begin with, I couldn't imagine her leaving Kyoto without telling me.

The day after I talked to her landlord, her mother came up from the country, worried. She used a spare key to enter the apartment, but Naoko wasn't inside. From there, she went straight to the police to file a report. At that point, she began to treat me with growing suspicion. I felt crushed beneath the weight of the situation. The police asked me for information, but I had nothing I could tell them.

I remembered Amagi's words: *Oh, you'll be back.*

What had I handed over to him?

○

I called out a greeting as I stepped into Amagi's garden, but he didn't come to the veranda. A gray veil of clouds covered the sky. The mansion was as dark and quiet as ever, the only sound the rustling of the bamboo forest that clung to the back of the building.

Unable to wait calmly, I strode back out the gate. A lukewarm breeze was blowing, far too warm for February. The air stuck to my body with a clamminess exactly like the soup I had drunk a few days earlier. It smelled sweet.

Outside the gate, the road sloped steeply to the west. Each time I visited Amagi's house, I'd climbed up and down that hill.

Eventually, Amagi appeared at the bottom of the slope. He strolled idly toward me, his kimono carelessly disheveled. Dangling from one emaciated hand was the fox mask I thought had been burned. He looked up at me and smiled a dark, desolate smile.

As I watched, the surface of the street behind him began to rise up like the pile of a rug. At first, I didn't understand what was happening, but eventually it dawned on me that rain was falling. The edge of the storm must have been directly behind him. Eventually it caught up and engulfed him. I stood at the top of the hill watching Amagi merge with the edge of the storm and ascend the slope.

I greeted him in the pounding rain.

"So here you are," he said, water trickling from his hair.

He put his arm around my shoulder and guided me into his mansion. The rainwater soaking his body seeped into my own.

○

I went to Hourendou.

The sky was a clear, cold blue, and the wooden Budai statue was basking in the sun with a carefree smile. Behind the glass door, I saw Natsume stand up from her seat at the counter, looking happy. But when I pushed open the door, her smile vanished like water sinking into sand.

I sat down silently in a wooden chair and warmed my frozen hands over the heater. My stiff fingers tingled as the warmth returned to them. The inside of the shop was as cozy and quiet as if it were wrapped in cotton batting. Natsume disappeared into the back and returned carrying a tray of tea and bean jelly.

I sipped my tea and gazed at the jelly, which was as black as lacquer. I thought of the little black box that had appeared when I gently untied its silk wrapping, and of the vivid picture of a frog painted on it, and of Amagi's thin, birdlike hand as he drew the box toward him.

I told Natsume I was quitting my job at Hourendou. She squeezed her teacup between her hands and said with a smile,

"That's quite sudden." I lowered my head. In the distance, I could hear the recycling truck drive slowly past as its operator made his request for used paper over the loudspeaker.

"I'd like to ask you something," I said.

"What is it?"

"Why did you send me to Amagi?"

"I'm sorry. It must have been very unpleasant for you," Natsume said softly, looking me in the eye.

"That's not what I mean." I let out a quiet breath and caught her frightened gaze. "What did you receive from Amagi in exchange for me?"

The blood drained slowly from her face. It looked like a carved sculpture drifting to the bottom of the water.

"Did Amagi say something to you?" she asked, looking down.

"You won't tell me?" I asked. She shook her head, still looking down.

"I'm sorry. I can't."

"Why not?"

Between her palms, the teacup trembled slightly. She drew her brows together and looked at me with moist eyes.

"After you quit this job, you'll return to a life unconnected to Amagi and me. You'll probably never visit Hourendou again. If that's the case, it's best you hear nothing more."

With that, she stopped speaking.

I heard a motorcycle pass the shop. Once the sound died away, silence descended on Hourendou again.

I thought about the dozens of hours I'd spent since the previous fall sitting in this quiet room, talking to Natsume without ever growing bored. I watched the air shimmer above the heater to our side and remembered how warm I used to feel after scarfing down the sake lees she toasted for me.

"I liked you," I mumbled. "It's too bad."

"I'm sorry," she said, her gaze still on the floor. "I liked you, too."

I sipped my tea and glanced at the bright hustle and bustle outside the glass doors. The wooden Budai was smiling up at the blue sky. I thought of the other Budai who had gobbled down cakes and laughed merrily but who smiled no more. Natsume followed my gaze. She stared at the statue with moist, childlike eyes.

"Naoko's disappeared," I muttered. "I'm sure you know that."

Natsume stiffened.

"Amagi said he was no longer interested in negotiating. I don't have anything I can exchange for her."

She was silent.

"I need your help," I said.

A long interval passed. Finally, Natsume stood up and went into the back room. She returned with a round, gleaming black object. It was the tray Sunaga had given her on her birthday. The red goldfish shone with luster.

"I'm going to pay a visit to Amagi." She began wrapping the tray in a cloth.

Her face in profile was beautiful. Her long, slender back looked resolute. But now that her tears had dried, her eyes were empty.

"Would you mind walking with me partway?" she asked.

○

When we came to the hill leading to Amagi's mansion, Natsume lifted her hand to her brow, as if to block the sunlight. "The weather's good today," she said. "It's Setsubun, you know. The anniversary of my father's death."

"What should I do?" I asked.

"Please head back now and do exactly as I say."

I nodded.

She looked me straight in the eye as she continued. "After sunset, you will go to Yoshida Shrine. Be certain to enter from the east side. You must not make a mistake. You must not run, and you must not look behind you. Walk straight down the road into the festival. Then look for Naoko."

"She'll be there?"

"You must not give up until you find her. You must not leave the festival. When you find her, you will take her with you and immediately leave from the west. You must not let go of her hand."

"I understand. I'll do as you say," I said. She looked into my face and nodded. "What are you going to do?" I asked.

She smiled without answering. Then she bowed deeply and walked away.

I stood there, watching her form recede.

She walked up the long, steep hill, head bowed, clutching her cloth-wrapped bundle. Amagi's house was at the top, nearly engulfed by the bamboo grove. The area looked dark, as though it were submerged.

I wondered what Amagi was expecting, there in the depths of his dim house. It seemed to me that the webs he used to entangle people led inexorably to that mansion on the hill. There he sat, in his long, narrow, dark room, like a denizen of some demonic realm. Licking his thin lips, intoxicated by the narcotic of boredom.

I watched Natsume pass through his gate, and then I left.

○

I recalled my last visit to Amagi.

"I'll show you my magic lantern," he'd said, ushering me into the house. "I just know you'll like it."

I watched my breath congeal white in the air as we walked down the endless corridors. Several times, I saw a faint light flicker behind one of the paper screens lining the passages, but as soon as we were upon it, the room behind the screen would sink into darkness, as if someone had blown out a candle. We passed several screened-off rooms like this as we made our way into the depths of the mansion.

Amagi was wearing the fox mask.

Finally, we entered a large, nearly empty room. One by one, Amagi lit the peculiar magic lanterns in each of the room's four corners. The room filled with a reddish glow. The lights flickered as if they might go out, then abruptly came into focus. A crowded festival night rose before my eyes. I saw a familiar figure standing amid the throng of people. The figure was looking around uncertainly as if they were searching very hard for someone.

"Naoko!" I cried.

"I told you it was amusing," Amagi said.

I looked at him. The blurry red light of the festival lit up the expressionless mask. Suddenly, he blew out the magic lanterns. The festival, Naoko, all of it vanished into darkness. The only sound was Amagi's breathing from deep in the shadows.

"Please give Naoko back," I said.

"You don't have anything else I want," he said quietly, lighting a lamp. "Poor thing."

He took off the fox mask, revealing his emaciated, bluish-white face. It was a feeble, eerie, sad face. His eyes in their sunken sockets were as vacant as glass orbs. He glanced casually in my direction, but his gaze wandered aimlessly, as if I weren't even there.

"Please give Naoko back," I repeated. His eyelids fell shut like two heavy doors.

"Poor thing," he said, his head drooping on his thin neck.

○

I climbed Yoshida Hill and slipped into the crowds of the Setsubun Festival.

With packs of people pushing and jostling one another, the usually quiet shrine felt like a different world. Rows of stalls sent the aroma of roasted meat and sweets wafting into the darkness.

Trusting Natsume's instructions, I sorted through the faces of the people on the road, searching for Naoko.

The path leading from the shrine past the front gate of Kyoto University to Higashioji Street was also buried under waves of festival-goers. Children happily stuffed their mouths with snacks, carrying balloons and toys. University students strolled along in clusters. The lights from the stalls illuminated their faces, making them look warm and cozy, just as Natsume had described.

I saw a few of my university friends in the crowd and pulled my scarf up over my mouth, afraid they'd call out to me. As I passed the stalls with their candy apples, cotton candy, and prizes, I began to wonder how I would ever find one woman among the push and shove of this enormous crowd.

Making my way through, I pulled out my cell phone and called Naoko. I could hear the ringtone I had heard so many times since she disappeared. Then I lowered the phone from my ear and listened carefully to the din of the festival. Beyond the sounds of people talking, food frying, and equipment creaking, I could hear the faint ringing of a bell. As I walked, the familiar sound grew gradually louder. I hurried toward it.

The sweet scent of pancake balls wafted toward me. There was Naoko. She was standing in front of the stall, gazing at it with soft, dreamy eyes. I could hear her phone ringing repeatedly inside her handbag.

I stood next to her and ordered a bag of pancake balls. She looked up at me in a daze but didn't say anything. Slowly, the light returned to her eyes, until she was staring in surprise at the sweets.

"Where am I?" she mumbled.

"Let's get out of here," I said.

As I took her hand and started walking, I thought I glimpsed a man in the crowd wearing a fox mask and a casual kimono. My heart pounded.

"What's the matter?" Naoko yelped quietly as I pulled her hand, starting to run.

I kept running with all my strength to escape the orange glow of the Setsubun Festival and return to the city. All the while I gripped her hand, not letting go until we reached Higashioji Street.

○

I haven't set foot near Hourendou since then. I don't know what happened to Natsume after she climbed the hill to Amagi's mansion, her cloth-wrapped bundle in her arms. Sometimes I imagine her on balmy days with her arms wrapped around the wooden Budai statue. But I can't go back to check.

Although some time has passed, now and then, I still have nasty dreams of being dragged back into the dusky shadows. Even when I manage to wake myself and break free from those dreams that seem to twine around my body, I feel as if they continue on. I lie staring up at the ceiling of my room, unable to move. Once or twice, I thought I saw a fox mask over Naoko's face as she reclined beside me, propped up on one elbow.

When that happens, I slowly drink a glass of water and stare at the fluorescent light until I can shake off the clinging dream. I try to push the memory of the fox man sitting in his dim room as far away as I can.

And I tell myself, Amagi is gone now.

○

I heard that Amagi died in his mansion.

He was found lying facedown in the center of that room at the back of the house. He had drowned. Next to him on the floor was a black tray, glistening moistly. There was nothing else in the room.

Supposedly, when his body was moved and his mouth pried open, a red goldfish tumbled out.

The Dragon in the Fruit

I remember the days when I used to visit a certain senior student from my university in his rooms and listen to him tell stories.

I remember his profile as he talked while warming his fingers over the electric heater, the low reading desk with the large black-leather notebook on it, the smell of the old books piled around the room, the thick smoke from his pipe curling around the lampshade—maybe it's because I had only recently started university and everything I came across in Kyoto was curious to me, but those images of my senior have a honeyed tint in my mind, as if they're sealed away in amber.

The particular weight of those memories sometimes makes me feel as if I spent most of my university days in his rooms, but the truth is, our friendship lasted only half a year.

By the spring of my sophomore year, he had vanished.

We never met again.

○

He was born at the base of the Shimokita Peninsula, in Aomori Prefecture. He told me his hometown was called Noheji. His family, once wealthy landowners, had been ruined by the postwar land reform. He had never left his hometown until graduating from high school, but he seized the opportunity offered by university to come to Kyoto. He had hardly returned home since. He was studying law. Between his sophomore and junior years, he'd taken off six months to travel the Silk Road, making it all the way to Istanbul. When I met him, he was studying for the bar.

That was all I knew about him in the beginning.

When we met, I was eighteen, and he was twenty-two.

○

We became friends through a humanities study group.

Since I'd just started university and was generally shy, I didn't have much chance to talk to him. It was summer before my shyness wore off and I got a sense of his personality, but right around then, he stopped coming to the meetings.

I wasn't intentionally copying him, but since the group wasn't as interesting as I'd hoped, I grew disappointed and stopped going myself. It was only after we both quit that we started talking on more personal terms.

About two weeks into second semester, I ran into him at Shiyou Shoin, a used bookshop on Takahara Street. Standing in a cramped, dim corner of the shop searching for a book, he looked rather lonely. He had none of the spirited drive I'd sensed when he held forth at our study meetings. I said hello, and he recognized me.

"Been to the study group lately?" he asked.

"No, I guess I got bored of it."

"That was fast," he answered with a smile.

The bookstore was very quiet, and the smell of old books seemed to have seeped even into his breath as he whispered. He didn't look at me, instead continuing to scan the shelves as we talked. When he wasn't speaking, he would reach up and stroke the spines of various books with his forefinger.

I saw him make that gesture many times in the months that followed. It was like he was absorbing a sense of the book through the touch of his finger on its spine. Later, when I started visiting him in his rooms and vaguely copying his behavior, I picked up the same habit. Even now, I sometimes notice myself lost in thought, stroking the spines of books on a shelf, and remember him.

"You come here often?" he asked.

"My rooms are behind this building."

We talked about books for a while.

I told him I was searching for Zweig's biography of Balzac, and he said he'd picked up a copy at the used book fair at Shimogamo Shrine. He invited me up to his rooms, saying he'd lend it to me.

○

My senior was an odd character.

He was studying law, but people said they'd spotted him going in and out of the engineering building, while others claimed to have seen him in advanced literature seminars. Aside from his dropping into the study group, no one seemed to know how he spent his time.

Acquaintances dreamed up all sorts of theories about his background. Some were entirely reasonable, and others sounded like ridiculous tall tales. He laughed them all off, refusing to say which were true and which were not. In contrast to these lively rumors, he himself was a quiet person. His mere presence produced a certain ambiance—even without doing anything unusual, he seemed to be drawing a line between himself and the rest of the world.

Although he didn't often say much, once he got started, the words welled up from him, as abundant as a bottomless spring. "Speaking of which," he'd say, and everyone would naturally gather round to listen.

When he talked, he would stroke the fingers of his left hand with his right forefinger one by one. Some people thought this odd gesture was his trick for remembering things. Considering his other habit of stroking book spines, they might have been right. And the way he seemed to know everything made you want to believe it. He could hold his own in debates with jazz fanatics, discuss haikus with literature students, expound on the development of ukiyo-e prints, or explain the various styles of gangster films.

Back when we were in the study group, I'd heard him reminisce about his past. I knew only fragments—his travels abroad, an antique-hunting American, a book-loving baker—but my interest was piqued. He had a great skill for turning his experiences into stories.

As I listened to him, I began to feel like a terribly boring, empty person. Other people must have felt the same way, and it seemed only natural that a few of them said, behind his back, that they were sick and tired of him.

When you've just started university, people only a few years older can seem like unbelievably experienced adults, but the impression my senior made on me was particularly strong.

○

His rooms were in an old two-story apartment building in Ichijoji. The Eizan Electric Railway ran right by it, and periodically the building would thunder with the sound of passing trains.

Stepping past the emergency staircase into the first-floor hallway, the damp-looking gray wall of the neighboring apartment loomed right in front of your nose, making the passage dark and dreary even at midday. Bundled newspapers, plastic bags stuffed with garbage, and cardboard boxes filled with junk lay messily outside the apartment doors. The dusty corpses of moths and crane flies dotted the corners of the bare concrete floor.

My senior rented two rooms in this building. One was for living in, and the other was for books—his library, so to speak.

The room measured four and a half tatami mats, and aside from the door, the walls were entirely covered by shelves. A shelf also blocked the lone window, preventing it from serving its purpose. The books overflowed from the shelves and were piled on the floor, leaving half the room with no space to walk. A sliver of floor had been carved out for a little antique-looking reading desk, which was covered in scraps of paper with notes jotted down on them, pen cases, and piles of books flagged with sticky notes. The room had a faintly sweet smell to it, which I later learned came from his pipe smoke.

It seemed to me like a comfortable prison with walls made of books. Although the books did not appear to be organized in any particular way, I never once saw my senior struggle to find something he was looking for.

That first day, I borrowed Zweig's biography of Balzac.

"Stop by anytime," he said. "I'm usually here."

I went back many times and spent many hours in his library. Sometimes I listened to his stories, and other times I read books from his shelves. While I read, he usually studied a guide to the bar exam or took sheets of writing paper one by one from a stack on his desk and ran his fountain pen across them. He didn't tell me what he was writing.

○

His wanderings had begun in the fall of his sophomore year and ended about six months later in Turkey. I didn't know why he decided to go on this long journey, but I liked hearing him talk about it.

He would pull the large black-leather notebook from its hiding place on the shelf and tell me stories as he flipped through it. Each page was meticulously filled out with a date, a map of the place he'd visited, and notes on the people he'd met and foods he'd eaten. It was a very detailed travel journal. He'd taken a boat from Kobe to Shanghai, and from there a train to Xi'an. That was the starting point of the Silk Road. He traveled through Dunhuang, Turpan, Urumqi, and Kashgar. There he boarded an international bus and crossed the border to Pakistan. He passed through Iran, then traveled across Turkey from east to west, headed for Istanbul.

"Turkey is a strange place. The only people there are kids and old men with long beards."

"Is that really true?"

"Wonder why that is. I guess when puberty ends, they jump straight to old age."

He used to play tricks on me like that.

Despite the fact that he'd gone on this long journey, as far as I knew, he almost never went out. When he did, it was either to go to the used bookstore or the movie theater, to buy food, or to bathe at the public bathhouse. I especially remember how much he liked the bathhouse.

The neighborhood bathhouse opened up around four. If we went then, there weren't many other customers, and we'd have the whole big place to ourselves, lit up by the evening sun. He loved to go for a bath at that hour and often did. On days when my classes ended early, I'd go along.

In a corner of his room, he kept a round wooden pail filled with everything he needed for the bath, and when he decided to go, he would happily tuck it under his arm. Locking up his room, he'd say in a singsong voice, "Off to the bath, off to the bath!" Then he'd slip on a big pair of wooden sandals and clop merrily across the asphalt to the bathhouse, his pail under his arm and a little white towel he'd gotten from a newspaper salesman over his shoulder. I'd walk next to him, dangling my own bath things in a plastic bag.

Soaking in the hot water put him in an excellent mood, and he talked more freely than usual. When the old men from the neighborhood, thin as pins, sat imposingly nearby, he'd keep quiet, but when no one else was there, he rambled on endlessly while we soaked.

"The droplets that drip down from the ceiling are cold, cold, cold…"

He would make up all sorts of odd little songs.

Occasionally, a woman would join us on these trips.

Usually, he treated her brusquely, but at the bathhouse, he turned boyish. When it came time to get out, he would shout over the wall between the men's and women's bath: "I'm getting out!" If she didn't answer, he would repeat himself more loudly. Eventually, he would start calling her by name, at which point she would give in and answer quietly, "Fine, fine."

Once, she said to him, "I wish you'd stop that."

"If we don't get out at the same time, one of us might catch a cold," he answered.

I thought he should let his playful side show more often. Even though she put on an annoyed face, she seemed to enjoy it.

My senior called her by her last name, Yuuki, and I called her by her first, Mizuho.

Mizuho was the same age as him, a graduate student in science. She was slender and tall, a little taller than me. She had narrow, intellectual eyebrows. When she talked, she had a habit of drawing them together and staring into the eyes of whomever she was talking to. Although she seemed busy with her research, she rarely let her tiredness or irritation show. She was always as calm as if she was standing beneath a fine, light rain.

At the time, I didn't know how the two of them had met. I figured they'd known each other for quite a while, but I didn't know if they met in university or earlier. Neither of them spoke much about their relationship, and I didn't try to force the information out of them.

I met her for the first time shortly after I began visiting my senior's rooms. I knocked as usual and went into the library. He was writing. I assumed he was alone but quickly realized a woman was sitting in the corner, reading a book. She was like a splash of color in that drab world. She had been scowling at the pages of a foreign book with her narrow eyebrows drawn together, but when she saw me, the tension in her face relaxed.

She smiled and politely said hello.

○

One day, my senior and I went on a long walk, something we rarely did.

The trees shading the streets were starting to change color, and as the sun set, a cold autumn wind began to blow. The sky was a clear, dark blue with a haze of red lingering in the west. The two of us walked over Yoshida Hill as darkness fell. We walked down the east side, through the grounds of Shinnyodo Temple, and came out on Shirakawa Street. Across from the rows of city buses at Kinrin Garage was a small used bookstore called Ryokuudou.

My senior knew the used bookstores of Kyoto well and had worked as a clerk at this one for a period. It was already closed when we got there, so we climbed the stairs on one side up to the café on the second floor. We sat at a table overlooking Shirakawa Street and ordered dinner.

"I was working at Ryokuudou when I met that book-loving baker," he said as we drank our after-dinner coffee. "He owned a business selling Western desserts. He's got two shops over in Yonjo. I've bought cake there before. He sells those cute little pastries, but he's this incredibly scary guy with a face like a beast. He even had a sword displayed in the alcove in his house. Weird guy."

Apparently, this baker was a regular customer at Ryokuudou and would show up two or three times a month.

He always stopped his shiny black car on Shirakawa Street and pushed open the glass door with a sour face. The owner of the bookstore would meet him with a frown. They were an intimidating pair, so when the two of them talked in hushed voices, a menacing aura would descend over the shop. But the truth was, all they ever talked about was books. Casual chitchat didn't exist between those two.

My senior had even visited this customer's house in his role as assistant to the bookstore owner. Since the owner didn't like driving, my senior took his place, operating a small truck. The baker lived in a newly built mansion north of Shimogamo Shrine. My senior would be invited into the living room, where he would set about pricing the books piled on the floor. The baker was a voracious reader who chewed through books at a superhuman speed. While my senior was busy pricing, the baker would sit cross-legged on the sofa and finish off one or two volumes. "Take these with you, too," he might say afterward.

"People who read that fast don't seem to be reading very seriously. They look like they're just flipping through the pages for fun."

"You read pretty fast yourself," I said.

"I'm nothing compared to him. He had a special gift."

"Is that how it works?"

"After I'd been there a few times, he apparently started to trust me, even though I'd never said much. Eventually, he asked me to do a job for him on the side."

I knew my senior had worked at secondhand shops and bookstores and as a tutor, but he said the work for the book-loving baker was the strangest he'd ever done.

"It looked almost like he was skipping town in the middle of the night. He told me to bring the truck over around midnight and not to ring the bell. When I got to the front of the house, I was supposed to wait for further instructions."

I was taken aback. "I can't believe you said you'd do it."

"I was curious."

"I could never do that. I'd be too scared."

"It was definitely scary."

"So what did you move for him?"

"I stopped the truck by the side of the road and waited. Before long, the baker emerged from the dark house. He was wearing a black suit. I got out of the car and went into the house. There was a lot to bring out. Most of it was packed up in boxes or wrapped in cloth...probably antiques he'd collected. That night, he planned to take them somewhere and sell them off. Most mysterious was an object like a bathtub. It was unbelievably heavy. We used a hand truck to bring it out, but we had a hell of a time hoisting it up on the truck bed with just the two of us. I wasn't sure what it was, since it was wrapped in tarps, but it stank of fish."

After they finished loading everything, my senior and the baker got in the truck. They drove through the dark residential streets to Shimogamo-Hondori Street. The truck with its strange cargo traversed the empty night streets. The baker didn't say a word, signaling with nothing more than a pointed finger when it was time to turn.

They drove north on Shimogamo-Hondori, then turned east on Kitaoji Street. They crossed the Takano River and drove through the Takano intersection to Shirakawa Street. From there, their route became more complicated, and my senior turned at many dark corners, pushing deeper into the mazelike neighborhood. Because the back alleys were so tangled and dimly lit, he couldn't be sure how he'd gotten there. With all the repeated turns, he didn't even know which direction was which. He remembered only a fragmented series of impressions: a lonely streetlight shining next to a rice field, a vending machine, houses with closed shutters, a dark drainage channel. They seemed to have come quite far, and he began to feel uneasy.

"It seems he took a roundabout way on purpose," he said.

They eventually arrived at an old mansion behind an imposing gate at the top of a steep hill.

A lantern glowed orange under the gate. My senior stopped the truck in front, as he was told. A moment earlier, no one had been there, but now, next to the lantern, he noticed a man standing at ease in a casual kimono. The baker silently gestured for my senior to stay where he was, got down from the passenger seat, and walked over to the waiting man.

"I watched them in the side mirror. The baker had a sort of scary look on his face. As for the man standing outside the mansion talking business, I have no idea what kind of face he was making, because he was wearing a fox mask."

"That's bizarre."

"The lantern under the gate was the only source of light—the mansion was pitch-black. There seemed to be a bamboo grove nearby, and it rustled the whole time we were there. After I sat for a little while, spacing out, the baker signaled me to help unload the truck. The man in the fox mask stood by watching us."

"Then what?"

"That was all for that night. After we unloaded the truck, we drove back to the baker's house. Before I left his place in Shimogamo, he paid me generously. I didn't have to work for a while after that."

None of the mysteries had been solved, and I felt let down. He lit his pipe and blew out a mouthful of smoke.

"I like that sort of thing," he said.

"What sort of thing?"

"Weird stuff like that. My experiences are nothing special, but over these five years in Kyoto, some mysterious things have happened."

"I haven't even experienced one mysterious thing yet. Actually, you're the most mysterious thing that's happened to me."

He smiled and glanced out the window. Shirakawa Street had disappeared into the indigo dusk. His thin face was reflected hazily in the window glass. I followed his gaze outside.

"When the sun sets and the lamps come on in the streets, I often think about all the people living in this city. Most of them are strangers, but I know they're connected by mysterious threads I can't even imagine. And when I have the chance to touch one of those threads, it makes a strange sound under my fingers. I think that if I could trace them all to their source, they would lead to a mysterious, shadowy place at the very core of the city."

He let out another puff of smoke and smiled.

"Of course, that's only a pipe dream."

○

"On short summer nights, in between the rice paddies, the foxes scatter," my senior intoned out of nowhere.

Outside, the sun seemed to have set. Since the window in my senior's library was blocked by a large bookshelf, very little light found its way inside. Quite often on my visits, I failed to notice that hours had passed and the night was far advanced. He would stand up, saying, "It's the middle of the night already," and take me over to the little Chinese restaurant next to his apartment building. When it was this late, all the other cheap restaurants were closed.

When he mumbled that strange line, I looked up from the book I was reading. He put down his bar exam study guide and turned toward me.

"Between the paddies?" I asked.

"On those narrow, raised footpaths, I'd guess," he muttered.

"That reminds me," he then continued, "I used to know a guy who worked with me making self-published literary magazines. He was the son of a priest at a temple in the Kamigyo Ward, and during summer vacation, he used to get the neighborhood kids together in the temple's main hall for tutoring sessions. It was more efficient than teaching them one-on-one in their houses. He didn't charge much per kid, but since there were a bunch of them, he said he made pretty good money. He invited me to stop by, so I did. The temple was down a back alley near Goryo Shrine, and it was much more impressive than I'd expected. The main hall was mysteriously cool even in midsummer, which made it perfect for studying. I helped him out with the tutoring and read some books. He was the type who always had creative ideas. He'd buy a bunch of *ramune* soda or orange juice, and when the kids' attention started to wander, he'd bring out the drinks. At lunchtime, too, there'd be food at the temple. I had time on my hands, so I used to help boil *somen* noodles and stuff like that in the huge temple kitchen."

"Sounds like camp."

"He taught kids from elementary school through junior high, so it was pretty lively."

"Must've been hard to find students."

"They were all junior students attending the same kendo dojo as he did. It was an old place called Seifuukan next to the temple. And he'd spent quite a few years there wielding his bamboo sword. I went there to practice with him a couple of times myself. I studied kendo in my hometown through junior high, so it was a real trip back in time."

"You did kendo? That's hard to imagine."

"I wasn't any good at competitions, but I was great at practice swings."

He pretended to grip a bamboo sword and swing it.

"One of the junior high girls who studied at the temple had a reputation for being good at kendo. She was smart and attentive, and she always stayed till the end of the study sessions, so my friend and I often walked her home. After all, there were reports of a phantom attacker in the area back then, so sending a junior high girl home by herself in the evening would've been a bad idea. She told us a lot of interesting things on those walks, like how to improve at kendo. But the most fascinating story of all was the one about the creature with the long body."

My senior paused to take a breath and pour some steaming-hot coffee.

"She said the creature made its home in abandoned old houses and wandered around aimlessly after dark. When she was in elementary school, she had seen it coming in and out of an empty house in her neighborhood. It looked sort of like a fox, but its torso was long and slithery like a serpent. As she stood by the side of the road staring at it, the creature turned toward her and snapped open its mouth. Its teeth were incredibly humanlike. She said it looked like it was giving her a toothy grin there in the gloom." My senior spoke as if telling a scary story. I smiled as I listened.

"It was probably a weasel. Animals turn up in the most unexpected places, you know."

"Even so, her story was both creepy and compelling. Perfect for testing one's courage. That's why, on the way back from her house, my friend and I decided to sneak into the abandoned building where she'd spotted it."

"Curiosity got you again, huh?"

"Nothing scary happened that time—we got covered in dust and didn't see any strange creatures. But after that, there was some trouble. At the end of August, a friend of the priest's son who belonged to a film club asked if he could use the temple grounds for a shoot. The priest's son thought it sounded interesting, so he got permission from his dad to do it.

"I remember very clearly the day the film club guys brought their equipment over. I was sitting on the veranda of the main hall watching them. The priest's son was very excited because they'd agreed to let him make a special appearance in the film. He didn't have any lines—he just crossed the set from right to left as an extra.

"After they finished filming the scene, we decided to watch it in one of the temple's rooms while we ate some watermelon and relaxed. The instant the priest's son saw it, he went white as a sheet. Then he keeled over, and there was a huge fuss. That day, I was so caught up in the chaos, what with calling an ambulance and all that, I never learned what happened. The priest's son developed a high fever and was confined to his bed."

My senior touched a lit match to the tobacco in his pipe and sucked in.

"At the beginning of September, I finally got a message that his condition had improved, so I went to the temple to see him. I still remember the way the whole sky was covered with clouds, except for a rift in the west where the sun shone through. There was a strange, reddish cast to everything. You know that painter De Chirico? The grounds of the temple felt like one of his paintings. Lonely, with no one around.

"I walked through the gate toward the temple. The main hall was in front of me, and my friend's house was on the left. I was heading in that direction when something long and slender slipped from under the floor of the main hall and slithered across the vacant grounds. It headed away from me to the right. As I stood there in shock, it suddenly stopped moving. I saw it raise its head like a snake preparing to attack, then look back toward me. It was hard to see because it was in the shadow of the main hall. But even in the shadows, its teeth were unmistakable. I could have sworn it turned toward me and snapped its mouth open in a smile.

"My friend was well enough to walk around by then, and that evening we went out for dinner together. That was when I learned for the first time that he had been tormented by all sorts of strange happenings ever since the two of us had poked around the abandoned house. He would hear beast-like growling at the end of the hallway late at night, or he'd wake up in the morning to find animal hair strewn around under the bedcovers. He'd been stewing over it on his own because he was too embarrassed to tell anyone else.

"That was when he saw the film clip. The scene took place on the temple grounds in midday. He passed through the frame from right to left. To us, he looked the same as always. But he told me that when he saw himself, he had the face of the creature."

He took a sip of his coffee.

"It sounds like he got pretty obsessed," I said.

"Maybe... But then what was it I saw on the temple grounds?"

"A weasel, I'm sure. It just looked strange because it was twilight."

"I wonder..." He smiled mischievously. "Around the time it started to get cold, I ran into the girl who'd told me about the strange creature. She was wearing a navy kendo uniform with her equipment bag over her shoulder and standing stock-still way down the street, staring at me. I didn't know why. When I got closer, she whispered, 'Teacher,' and kept staring at me. I asked why she was giving me such a scary look. She replied, 'When you turned the corner a second ago, your face looked like the face of some huge creature.' Then she walked off, cackling."

As we sat there staring at each other in silence, my senior's little room seemed to sink into the late-night quiet.

"On short summer nights, in between the rice paddies, the foxes scatter," he recited softly. "For some reason, the poem reminds me of that summer."

Our stomachs were grumbling. It was after eleven.

Just as we were talking about going out for a bite to eat, Mizuho showed up. She was on her way home from a drinking party with her lab mates and was happily tipsy, which was rare.

That night, the three of us went together to the local Chinese restaurant.

○

The fall leaves at Kiyomizudera were lit up for the season, and the mountains that loom over the city's east side had taken on the warm red and gold hues of autumn. The weather was growing colder, with the kind of chill that accumulates steadily in the ground. It was my first winter in Kyoto.

The university held its annual festival, but I took no part in it. I did let a friend use my name on his application to set up a stall. But otherwise, I spent all my time in my senior's rooms.

On bitterly cold nights, he would pull some books off the shelf and take out a bottle of alcohol he had stashed behind them. I drank whiskey for the first time in his rooms. I found the taste unpleasant, but even so, I enjoyed sitting with a little blanket over my shoulders, sipping my drink and listening to his stories. He would put a blanket over his shoulders, too, and chew on his brown pipe, periodically exhaling puffs of sweet-smelling smoke.

The topics flew by with dizzying speed.

He told me about strange books he'd come across while working at the used bookstore, about his showdown with a group of guys who were blackmailing people at school on the orders of a woman called "the Queen," about a curio shop called Hourendou that the book-loving baker had introduced him to and an incident there involving trafficked goods, about the film he'd made with a group of friends to submit to a film festival and the weird, complicated conflicts that took place during the filming. After he'd talked about his university exploits for a while, he would move on to childhood memories and stories of his hometown.

It was on just such a night that he told me how he fell in love with books.

"Were you one of those kids who always loved to read?" he asked me.

"My parents were big readers, so I took after them. Was your family like that?"

"Not at all. My father hated anything between two covers. But you know how kids are—that only made me more curious about them."

He said his family didn't keep any books or magazines in the house.

There had been a large collection of old books in their storehouse, stockpiled by his grandfather, but his father sold off every last one. His father detested books. Therefore, to his children, books became all the more mysterious and alluring. My senior was the youngest of four siblings, and his oldest brother was the first to start reading. This brother spoiled him more than any of their other siblings and would pass on his books for him to read.

But their father found out about the older brother's books and made him burn them. Their father watched from the veranda as his brother threw the books onto a fire in a corner of the garden. My senior said the image of this bonfire of books he'd witnessed as an elementary student was etched forever into his memory.

His father and older brother were estranged for a long time. One year, after a lengthy quarrel, the two of them flew into a rage at each other. His father picked up a short sword that had been hanging in the alcove as a decoration and started swinging it around. Only after my senior put him in a full nelson did order return to the house.

After that, his brother moved to Kyoto to attend university.

Eventually, he followed in his brother's footsteps, though by then he didn't know where his brother was, as he'd severed contact with their family while he was still in university.

○

The living quarters next to my senior's library contained very little furniture.

There was a small refrigerator, a kitchen cupboard, and an electric heater and fan he left out all year. In fall and winter, the blades of the fan grew white with dust. The absence of furniture left the stained, dingy walls fully exposed, which made the room extremely dreary. Even though it was only four and a half mats, it felt bigger than my own six-mat room. If the library next door was a comfortable prison, this was like one of those old-fashioned rooms for confining lunatics. My senior didn't even lock the door, because, he said, there was nothing to steal.

In one corner of the room was his folded-up futon and, next to that, a small lamp, a book to read in bed, and his traveling bag. I think the lack of furniture wasn't the only reason the room felt so lonely—it was that bag. Every time I looked at it, I got the feeling he had already finished preparing for his next journey.

One night, I told him as much, and he shook his head.

"I've had enough traveling. Once in a lifetime is enough for that sort of thing..."

"But it still makes me feel that way. Without any furniture, it looks like you're just about to move."

"Can't be helped. All I do in here is eat and sleep."

"Do you always keep that bag by your bed?" I asked, pointing to the old pouch. He smiled wryly.

"That doesn't have traveling gear in it, just some old junk. It's where I keep everything I don't know what to do with, so I don't have to worry about it every time I move. Letters from my older brother, a pipe I bought at a bazaar, a hat. The short sword my dad once waved around is in there, too."

"Sentimental stuff, then?"

"Stuff like that serves no real purpose. And it's so annoying to worry about whether to keep it or throw it out," he said. Then he ate something he called "easy ramen." I don't think it was much more than a soup made from cheap chicken meat and green onions seasoned with soy sauce and chili oil, but when he put in a package of those fresh noodles they sell at the supermarket, it made a simple, delicious meal.

He rambled on about the pirates of Lake Biwa, about Nagahama Castle and Toyotomi, Hideyoshi, and moved from Kunitomo

Ikkansai all the way to steam locomotives before settling into a discussion of the Lake Biwa Canal. He described long-ago events of the Meiji era in great detail, explaining just what a huge project the canal had been.

"I've got a book about it," he said, showing me a volume authored by one of the project's planners, Tanabe Sakuro. "Pretty unusual, right? That book-loving baker gave it to me."

○

By early December, the autumn colors had faded, and instantly Kyoto was bursting with Christmas decorations. When I was a kid, I used to celebrate Christmas with my family, but once I was living on my own as a student, I didn't see much point in it. I hadn't been planning to do anything special, but my senior invited me to spend it with him.

"Yuuki's coming over, so why don't the three of us celebrate together?"

This was a surprise, since I had assumed he wouldn't bother with Christmas. But if he was going to have a special evening with Mizuho, then I didn't want to be the third wheel. I turned him down at first, but then she called me and told me I should join them. "And would you buy some fried chicken on your way over?" she asked.

On Christmas Eve, the day of the party, I showed up at my senior's rooms with a box of fried chicken. He'd put away the stacks of books in the library to make room for a folding table and covered it with a white tablecloth. I placed the box of chicken on top, and he lit a large red candle. When we turned off the lights, the candle illuminated the bookshelves encircling us.

"Looks like an alchemist's workshop," my senior said, sounding pleased.

The two of us gazed at the candlelight for a while before Mizuho arrived with a bottle of red wine and some glasses in a paper bag. She let out a gasp of delight at the scene. Normally she was cool and collected, but she had the excitement of a little girl when she sat down in front of the candle. "It looks like Christmas!" she exclaimed. She pulled the cork out of the wine and poured three glasses.

"He wouldn't come when I invited him. But when you invite him, it's a different story," my senior said. "In the end, that's life."

I waved away his suggestion. "I was just being polite."

"Most people are like that," Mizuho said.

I gave my senior a sheaf of cream-colored writing paper. Mizuho gave him an old map of Kyoto and me a scarf. My senior apparently hadn't expected to receive any gifts. He pondered the situation for a moment, then went over into the other room and came back holding a little stone and a black notebook. He gave me the notebook and Mizuho the stone.

The stone was about the size of a walnut with a soft, milky-white color. When she turned it around in the candlelight, it shone like it was wet. She gazed at it in the palm of her hand and sighed quietly. I peered at it from beside her. This was no ordinary stone nestled so neatly in the palm of her hand. It was a beautiful carving of a tiny dragon curled up in what looked like a persimmon, with its face peeping out.

"When the owner of Ryokuudou found out I'd done some work for the book-loving baker, our relationship soured, and I ended up quitting my job at the bookstore. After that, I got a job at Hourendou, the curio shop in Ichijoji. I didn't end up working there long, because I left on my travels six months later, but I became quite close with the owner, a fellow named Sunaga."

He said Sunaga gave him the carving before he left on his trip. It was called a netsuke.

In the past, people used to carry medicine and things around in little pillboxes, and the netsuke was used to attach the box to the obi of a person's kimono. Netsuke production reached the height of sophistication in the Edo period. Needless to say, these old carvings were now very expensive and not so easy to obtain. I had no idea how much the "dragon in the fruit" resting in Mizuho's palm might be worth.

But she quietly held it out to my senior. Her expression in the faint candlelight was tense. "I don't need this," she said.

"You don't have to be polite," he said.

"I don't need it."

The mood in the room became awkward and stiff. As he looked at Mizuho, my senior had an offended expression that I hadn't seen before. Since he didn't reach out to take the netsuke, she seemed unsure what to do with it, finally setting it beside the candle. She lowered her gaze, keeping her face cast down for a while.

At the time, I didn't know if what I had just witnessed was the start of an ordinary lover's quarrel or something else. Mizuho wasn't the type to get upset in front of me, so I assumed she must have a very compelling reason for her actions.

Mizuho kept looking down, and my senior remained silent, looking away from her. The frozen atmosphere did not seem likely to melt anytime soon. I made up an excuse and stood to head home. As I left the room, I glanced back once more at the pair, softly illuminated by the candlelight.

My senior sat cross-legged, stroking the spines of a stack of books beside him, while Mizuho sat with her legs tucked under her, head bowed, unmoving.

○

With Christmas over, the city changed its appearance once again as the New Year approached.

I had plans to return home on the twenty-eighth, so on the night of the twenty-seventh, I stopped by my senior's rooms. It wasn't quite a year-end party, but the two of us went out to an *izakaya* in Sanjo. He said he didn't go out drinking near the university because it was annoying to run into people from school.

"I'm sorry you got caught up in that awkward situation the other night," he said, bowing his head as he poured me a drink. "That kind of thing happens with her sometimes."

He didn't explain in any more detail.

I changed the subject, asking him what sort of work he did at Hourendou. He told me about setting up a stall at an antiques market and going to the warehouse of a mansion in Kitashirakawa. The alcohol loosened his tongue. I was drunk, too, and in a pleasant mood as I listened.

The *izakaya* was packed with a lively crowd. The table next to ours, a mixed group of foreigners and Japanese, was especially loud. My senior suddenly looked up and fixed his gaze on one of the foreigners in the group. When they finally got up to leave, he watched them go with an amused smile.

"One of the people with them was an American who often came to the curio shop," he said. "I haven't seen him in quite a while. He's still living in Kyoto, I guess."

We moved to a little bar in Kiyamachi and kept drinking.

"He said he was from San Francisco. He made his living by teaching English conversation and exporting Japanese antiques to the United States. He bought a lot of dubious items from Hourendou. But he wasn't an antique collector or anything so overblown as that. He liked things made in the Japanese style with an interesting appearance, and he didn't care if they were fakes. He had a friend in San Francisco with a store selling Japanese knickknacks and apparently worked as a buyer for this friend. Hourendou wasn't a particularly intimidating shop to visit, so it must have been convenient for him, though apparently he preferred visiting rummage sales to hunt around for good finds."

My senior took a bite of grilled sausage.

"His father had been in Kyoto right after the war ended. When the American Army came to Japan, the occupation set up a base here. He said his father had an interest in antiques and used to stop by various curio shops whenever he went out on the town. He told me some of the stories he'd heard from his father, and a lot of them were really wild. Made me think his father had been putting him on. I remember he really wanted to see a magic lantern."

"Aren't those things all over the place?" I asked. He shook his head.

"This was something his father had seen at the mansion of a businessman who lived along the canal, and it was no ordinary magic lantern. There were four parts to it, and when you placed them at set points around the room, a three-dimensional creature would appear in the center. This supernatural being apparently performed all sorts of motions. The owner of the curio shop said he'd never heard of anything like it. I looked into it myself but couldn't find anything."

"You think his dad made it up?"

"Could be he was spinning tales about the mysterious land of Japan for his son. That's quite the lie, though, since his son ended up actually coming here."

"If a magic lantern like that exists, I'd like to see it myself."

"He was searching for something else odd, too. It was another thing the businessman had shown his father—a taxidermy creature. Apparently, his father told him that every Kyoto household had one on display because it was considered good luck, which was obviously a total lie. Of course, there's plenty of sketchy stuff, like mummified water spirits and mermaids. But according to this American guy, the one his father saw had a long, snakelike torso. He said the body was all twisted around and the face with its bared teeth was somehow human-looking."

I suddenly remembered my senior's story about the spooky creature that had possessed his friend.

"That sounds a lot like the story you told me about the temple."

"Weird, right?"

"Did you ever find out the truth about the stuffed creature?"

"No, I never did. But he was grateful for my investigative efforts, and we became friends. He even invited me to some get-togethers at his house. He'd renovated a town house near Imamiya Shrine and was living there with some friends. He threw great parties, and his guests were always interesting. Unfortunately, I've always been bad at foreign languages." My senior smiled. "That's where I met Tenmaya."

I cocked my head at him, feeling tipsy. I'd never heard that name before.

"Who's Tenmaya? That's a new one for me."

"Tenmaya is a street performer. Someone I respect," my senior replied. "I told you I had a companion on my Silk Road travels, didn't I? That's who it was."

"If you respect him, he must really be something."

"He is. He's a great guy. And he's my older brother."

He grinned at my surprise.

We left the bar in Kiyamachi and stamped down the street on drunken feet. Although it was late as we crossed the Shijo Bridge over the dark Kamo River, the streets were still crowded. Since it was already past midnight, we decided to take the Keihan Railway home.

As we left Demachiyanagi Station and started down the quiet streets, my senior, a vague loneliness in his voice, asked, "So you're going back to your hometown tomorrow?"

"Aren't you going back to Aomori?"

"I'm not sure. It doesn't really matter to me."

"You ought to go back."

We parted ways in front of my lodgings on Takahara Street. It was eerily quiet this late at night, with only the line of white streetlights floating, suspended in the darkness.

"Good night," he said, raising a hand before heading north down the dark street.

"Happy New Year," I called as I watched him go.

He turned back and looked at me, then let out a soft cry.

"What's wrong?" I asked.

He was standing under a streetlight, staring at me. His face was lit up eerily by the white light above. He didn't answer, so I asked again, "What's wrong?"

"Nothing, it's just that your face looked like some kind of creature—"

A shiver ran down my spine. "That's creepy. Please don't say that," I said.

"Sorry."

With that, he turned on his heel and walked off at a quick pace.

○

After the New Year, second semester neared its end and finals began. Since I'd skipped more than half my lectures in second semester, I had to rely on the few friends I had in my department to get through the tests.

In late winter and early spring, I always think about the coming year. I get the urge to reflect on the past, even if it's unpleasant. I regretted spending so much time at my senior's place and ignoring everything else, and I told myself I needed to establish some distance. When I stopped visiting his rooms, my free time opened up, and I filled it with jobs I chose at random. Even if I couldn't go on a grand adventure like he had, I figured it wasn't a bad idea to do something on my own. I took a part-time position at a brewery in Tanbabashi, got a gig setting up for concerts, and worked the night shift at an inn in Sanjo.

My senior and Mizuho called several times, but I turned down their invitations.

○

On the night of the Setsubun Festival at Yoshida Shrine, Higashi Ichijo Street was packed with stalls, and Yoshida Hill bustled with people. I had finally accepted one of my senior's invitations, agreeing to meet him at a café in Hyakumanben on my way home from work in Osaka. When I arrived, he and Mizuho were sitting across from each other, staring silently out the window at Imadegawa Street. My senior smiled happily when he saw me.

"It's been a while. You've been hard to get ahold of."

"I've been busy."

"He doesn't live a life of leisure like you," Mizuho said.

"That was rude. I'm extremely busy, you know."

After a cup of hot coffee, we headed for Yoshida Shrine.

Setsubun is the coldest time of year in Kyoto, and that night it snowed. At first, there was only a dusting, like confetti. But as we advanced toward the main shrine building down the alley of stalls, each cocooned in warm air, it began to fall in earnest, blotting out our surroundings like white smoke. The bulbs in the stalls illuminated the pine trees on either side of the path so that they seemed to float up from the depths of the darkness, and wind-blown snow danced in the light. Everyone on the path was smiling as the snow piled up on their heads and shoulders.

Swaddled in a big scarf, my senior made his way through the crowd, his face a childlike expression of amazement. Now and then, Mizuho raised her hand to brush the snow from my hair. "You'll catch cold," she said. My senior kept stopping in front of the stalls, lured by the gusts of steam rising from them. Mizuho said she had a craving for pancake balls, so he bought her some.

Suddenly, he stopped short. I glanced over to see what had caught his eye. He was staring at a toy fox mask hanging from the display rack at one of the stalls.

As we followed the shrine road east from Higashi Ichijo to Yoshida Hill, the crowd grew increasingly dense. The firewood piled on the shrine grounds was going to be lit at eleven, and onlookers were gathering in front of the main shrine to watch.

"It's not much fun with so many people," my senior said. We continued past the main shrine on a path that led toward the back side of Yoshida Hill. Normally it was a lonely stretch, but tonight it, too, was lined with stalls and thronging with festival-goers. We bought paper cups of *nigorizake* and walked along, slowly sipping the cloudy alcohol. My senior and Mizuho were passing one cup back and forth between the two of them.

"Tenmaya used to perform at festivals like this," my senior said, watching the crowds come and go as he sipped his drink.

"That reminds me, I never heard the rest of your story about him."

"After I became friends with the American customer of that curio shop I told you about and began spending time at his house, I met all sorts of people. His conversation students would visit, as well as quite a few foreigners living in Kyoto. But the most unusual of all was said to be a man called Tenmaya. This man had belonged to a group of street performers in university and ended up making a living of it. Sometimes he would show up at the American's parties.

"I finally had a chance to meet him when the American invited me to an Easter party. One glance and I was in shock. The man called Tenmaya was my older brother. He had left home for university years earlier, and since he cut off contact with my family while he was in school, I hadn't known where he was.

"The night we first met, we stared at each other in silence. Far from feeling joy, I was so shocked by the encounter that I didn't know what to say. After all, there I was, far from home, supposedly meeting a mysterious street performer at the house of a foreigner living in Kyoto, and it turns out to be my brother. After a few moments, we both smiled, and soon we were laughing uncontrollably."

My senior downed the rest of his *nigorizake*.

A surge of excitement ran through the crowd near the main shrine, signaling that the bonfire had been lit, but the path was too crowded to head back. We decided to go down the east side of Yoshida Hill and head home. By the time we reached Kaguraoka Street, the neighborhood was so peaceful, it seemed we must have imagined the energy of the festival. The snow swirled in the light of the lamps lining the street. It wasn't coming down quite as hard now.

"My brother used to stop by my rooms now and then to tell me what he was up to. That's how I heard about his plan to travel the world. He invited me to come along, but I couldn't make up my mind to go. I'd just started living in Kyoto, and there was still a lot I wanted to see, and I had my classes to think about, too. I wasn't about to drop everything and leave the country, so I helped him out with his street shows for a while. He'd perform on those little stages in department stores or next to the Yonjo Bridge. I would bring in the crowd while he levitated."

"He can fly? That's incredible."

"He did lots of other acts, too. Have you heard of Kashin Koji?"

"You mean that magician from the 1500s?"

"What my brother did was sleight of hand, but he billed himself as a magician."

"Did you steal any of his tricks?"

"Not possible. I'm too clumsy." My senior smiled wryly. "Once the two of us went to a big mansion next to Ginkakuji Temple. It was an old place next to the Lake Biwa Canal, built in the Meiji period, and they were having a grand banquet. It was as lively as a little festival, with all sorts of odd characters. The master of the house himself was an eccentric and obsessed with dragons. Even the lamps in the garden were carved with the figure of a climbing dragon. My brother transformed a koi fish into a dragon and got a standing ovation. This man's support was part of what allowed my brother to take his trip. I went along, and that's how I ended up traveling the Silk Road."

Mizuho stopped in front of a vending machine and bought a can of hot coffee. She hugged it to her chest to warm herself. I bought one, too. Snow had settled on her hair, so I brushed it off. She thanked me, exhaling a puff of white breath. My senior stood in the shadows a few steps from the vending machine with his hands in his pockets and his chin buried in his scarf.

Mizuho pressed her can of coffee against her white cheek. "That kind of story bores me," she muttered.

"Bores you?" my senior echoed from the darkness.

"Yes, it bores me," she said and walked on ahead of us.

○

I was so busy running around starting new things without the least forethought that by the end of spring break, I was sick with a fever.

I'd started to feel ill one day as the train rumbled along on my way home from work at Osaka Castle Hall, and the moment I got to my room, I collapsed on my bed. I ran a low fever at first, but after some fitful sleep, my temperature shot up. I don't know how much time I passed in that delirious state. At one point, the door of my room opened. I stayed in my futon, unable to move. Someone walked over, crouched down by my pillow, and peered into my face. I heard a voice say, "Man, you look awful."

Later, my senior told me that he'd tried calling me a bunch of times while I was bedridden. When I finally answered, I raved feverishly at him. Suspecting something was wrong, he came to my apartment. He explained the situation to the building manager and got them to open my door, at which point he found me lying in bed. He bundled me into a taxi and took me to a nearby clinic. He paid my bill, too. Just waiting for my turn was such a struggle, I hadn't even thought about the bill.

After I took some flu medicine, he tucked me back in my futon and went to the convenience store to buy me some yogurt. "I put something to drink in the fridge. If you sweat a lot, make sure you change your clothes," he told me, peering into my face.

I huddled up in my futon. "I'm a boring person," I mumbled without context. The fever had made me feel weak, and I wanted to see what happened if I said it.

"I see," my senior said, nodding quietly. "I am, too."

Thanks to the flu medicine and my senior, I was able to crawl back from the fiery depths of hell. Apparently, my senior told Mizuho, because the next day, she stopped by to check on me. "I'm acting as proxy today," she said, making a pot of rice porridge with eggs and scallions.

We chatted a little as we ate the porridge. I let myself be more vulnerable around her and felt I could say things I couldn't say to my senior. I started talking about topics I'd had a hard time bringing up in the past. The reason I'd stopped visiting my senior's rooms was that I felt uneasy around him. I liked listening to his stories, but when I compared myself to him, I felt like a horribly boring human being. I told her I'd simply been unable to stand it anymore.

As I spoke, her face clouded over. I remembered her making the same expression on Christmas Eve and at the Setsubun Festival. I realized she was thinking about him.

She stared silently at her hands.

Finally, she said, "He's the boring one." Her words were cold, but there was no trace of irritation or anger in her tone.

"I don't think he's boring," I said. "It's me who's boring."

"Why is everyone so hung up on that? That's what's boring."

She stood and started washing the pot.

○

All at once, beneath the blue bowl of sky that covered Kyoto, the cherry trees burst into blossom.

A year had passed since I arrived in the city. I was in high spirits as I rode my bike below the boughs of the cherry trees lining Lake Biwa Canal. I'd taken a job three days a week at a bookstore near Ginkakuji Temple, and I'd started showing up for my classes, too. Nothing in particular had spurred this change. It happened naturally. The admission ceremony had taken place on April eighth, and the campus was overflowing with new students who reminded me of myself a year earlier.

I'd started visiting my senior's library again. Although I'd stayed away for a while, my senior and his room of books were exactly as I'd left them. Like before, I read, listened to his stories, and went with him to the bathhouse. It felt nostalgic to hear the *clip-clop* of his wooden sandals. The only difference was that Mizuho didn't come by very much anymore. I often thought of her expression the day she'd stopped by to check on me when I was sick. Her words echoed in my ears: *He's the boring one.*

On her birthday, my senior invited me to celebrate with the two of them.

"I'll pass," I said. "I've had enough of getting caught up in your arguments."

"This time we're just going out for dinner. It won't be like Christmas. I talked to her about it, too. She likes you."

On the night of her birthday, I went to my senior's rooms. As usual, he was flipping through books as he wrote. I took a volume off the shelf and began to read it. The time passed quietly, but Mizuho didn't come. Now and then, my senior looked up at the clock and frowned. When nine o'clock came and went, he muttered, "I don't think we can go tonight." He set down his pen and turned to me with a bitter smile. "Apparently, she's very busy."

He pulled out the bottle of whiskey hidden behind his books. I wasn't that hungry, but I still hadn't given up on the hope that Mizuho would show, so I sipped my glass prudently. My senior packed some of his favorite tobacco into his usual pipe and lit it. He swirled the smoke around at the front of his mouth. Each time he puffed, thick smoke rose from the dark-brown tobacco, sending a sweet scent through the room.

"I'll tell you about my grandfather," he said, holding the pipe between his teeth as he stroked his fingers.

That night, he told me the story of his grandfather, which was also the story of why his father hated books.

My senior was born into a family of landowners who had flourished after the Meiji Restoration. They were upstarts who rented to many smallholders and also operated as moneylenders. By the Taisho period, the family had a firm grip on power within the local community. However, the influence gained by earlier generations would not last forever, and just as their strength began to wane, they were devastated by the postwar land reform. My senior's grandfather had been the last pillar of strength supporting the family through this stormy period.

Around 1975, his grandfather turned sixty and decided to write his autobiography. Originally, he'd planned on selecting memories from childhood through the present to dictate, but as his ambitions swelled, he began talking about creating a record of the family's prosperous Meiji years. Then, as he began working toward this goal, he decided to trace their roots back even further. By the time family members realized something was amiss, his plans had already swerved off track into the haze of his deluded mind. He had become absorbed in fabricating a detailed history of the family's pre-Meiji exploits.

His room was piled with books and documents he had collected. There were family records dating from the Meiji period on, suspicious documents of questionable origin, cheap-looking collections of local myths, old articles, and copies of *The Chronicles of Japan* and *A Chronicle of Medieval Japan*. His grandfather would sit among these volumes, wholly absorbed in writing. His autobiography had transformed into a family story stretching endlessly on from the age of myth. His fantastical family history had been patched together from jumbled fragments, taken from those piles of documents without any consideration for coherence.

According to my senior's grandfather, the family descended from the cursed child who appears at the beginning of *The Chronicles of Japan*. Before the gods Izanagi and Izanami begot the Japanese archipelago, they gave birth to a mysterious child called Hiruko. *The Chronicles* tell of how this child was sent out to sea in a reed boat. In my senior's grandfather's story, the cursed child eventually washes up in the north of Japan, where he grows to adulthood. While the gods are battling among themselves in the west, Hiruko fathers many children, eventually establishing a dynasty. This dynasty represented the peak of Ezo culture and ruled the northernmost realms of Japan. The grandfather's story was full of legends of unknown origin, such as that the dynasty donated masses of gold from its mines to the Imperial Court for the construction of an enormous statue of the Buddha and that it helped Minamoto no Yoshitsune escape to the north. The dynasty's hold on northern Japan continued until it was broken up by Date Masamune at the end of the Warring States period. Even after this, the family line continued unbroken through the Edo period, enjoying its last burst of glory after the Meiji Restoration.

This was the fictitious family chronicle that emerged from the grandfather's wild delusions. In his mind, there was no line between historical fact and legend. He pieced together countless tales and false histories at random to weave together his long saga. As he discovered one new tale after the next, he fit them into the blanks in his imagined history.

When my senior was two years old, his grandfather's writing project was halted. His father, wild with frustration, shut him away and destroyed his entire storeroom of documents. That trove of books and papers, along with the scent of delusion that rose from it, were what made his father despise the written word.

As his grandfather neared the end of his life, my senior would visit him in the room at the back of the house where he was locked up and listen to his stories. He told me he still remembered the sound of his grandfather's hoarse voice as he fluently recounted the family history, stroking the ends of his fingers all the while. His grandfather had stored an exact copy of his "autobiography" in his mind and, even locked up in that room without pencil or paper, he continued to polish the manuscript, adding anecdotes here and removing them there. Eventually, my senior realized that the chronicle was no more than his grandfather's delusion, but he was still drawn to the fantastic tale. He was fascinated by the fact that this dizzyingly long history had been fashioned in such a way that it all led to him, the final link in the family line.

In the fall of my senior's first year of junior high, his grandfather died in his room at the back of the house.

"With his long, uncut white hair and his frame as thin as a skeleton, my grandfather looked like a demon living in that back room. His appearance was so frightening, none of his other grandchildren wanted to go near him. He didn't live in the real world. He lived in a world of his own creation."

I glanced at the clock. It was already after midnight. I felt as if I was finally returning to reality.

Mizuho never appeared that night.

I left my senior's library at one in the morning. As I closed the door, I saw him turn toward his mountain of books and begin to write. He was wholly absorbed in the notebook before him.

○

I met up with Mizuho at the Kyoto Municipal Museum of Art in Okazaki.

On the Keage Incline, petals drifted down from the cherry trees lining both sides of the old railroad tracks.

Mizuho had called me the day before and invited me out to make amends for standing us up on the night of her birthday. She said she wanted the two of us to meet without my senior, which made me suspicious. She had never asked to meet me alone in the past.

That day, I skipped class and headed to Okazaki. Several benches were lined up in the shade of the trees surrounding the museum, and Mizuho was sitting idly on one of them. The dry spring breeze ruffled her bangs. She didn't notice me until I was standing right next to her.

We walked through the museum's exhibits together.

In part because it was a weekday, hardly anyone else was there. The spring sunlight shone brightly through the windows into the deserted exhibition halls. As we looked at the paintings, I stole a few glances at Mizuho and noticed that she'd lost weight recently. She had a delicate frame to start with, so her figure didn't look much different, but her face was gaunt. Her eyes, too, looked as if her mind was somewhere else. If I didn't move on to the next painting, she probably would have stood in front of the same one endlessly, never getting bored. Although she gazed intently at the canvases, I wondered if she was seeing anything at all.

We left the museum and went into a small café on the grounds. She bought me lunch. We took a seat by the windows. The sunlight flooded in through the large plate glass, enveloping her face.

"I'm changing labs. I'll start before the end of April," she said, moving her spoon around. "I'm going to Tokyo."

"That's sudden."

"I'll be leaving soon."

"I hope you'll come back to Kyoto sometime."

"I might not. My family lives in Yokohama."

"That's a little cold of you. Will you and he keep things up long-distance?"

"I'm not worried about that." She smiled. "I'm leaving him, too."

After that, she talked about her research, looking even more mature than usual.

We finished our meal and went for a walk. From the municipal museum, we headed along Lake Biwa Canal toward Nanzenji Temple.

The spray of the fountain by the boat dock sparkled brilliantly in the spring sun. We walked down a little passageway to the Incline, emerging into a tunnel of cherry blossoms. Tourists were milling around the edges of the rusty railway tracks, looking up into the rain of petals. Beneath the trees, Mizuho was tinted light pink.

"I came here with him for a walk once," she said.

"To see the cherry blossoms?"

"I dragged him out of his room by force. We walked all around and came out by the aqueduct at Nanzenji. Know where I mean? You can follow the waterway from the Keage Power Station down to the temple."

"I've walked along there."

"That day, we stopped into a café near Nanzenji, and he found a notebook on one of the seats. It was the Silk Road journal. He's shown that to you, I'm sure. The owner's name and contact number were written in it, and I told him he ought to return it, but instead he shut himself up in his room and got completely absorbed in reading it. He even wrote notes in the margins." She smiled. "That was when it started."

She told me he'd actually been born in Hiroshima, in a town called Fukuyama. Both his parents were teachers, and he had one younger sister. Although he'd never left his hometown until graduating from high school, he'd seized the opportunity offered by university to come to Kyoto. He'd been home only occasionally since then. He studied law at school. He'd never traveled the Silk Road, and he hadn't worked at a used bookstore or a curio shop. Neither the antique-hunting American nor the book-loving baker nor the autobiography-obsessed grandfather nor the street-performer brother nor the mysterious man in the fox mask existed.

A breeze sent cherry petals dancing.

Mizuho plucked one from her hair and floated it on the wind.

"I'm sorry."

"Why are you apologizing? You're not the one who lied, are you?"

"Not about that. I'm apologizing for revealing his lies."

"I don't care about that." I thought for a moment, then added, "It doesn't matter if they're true or not. That's not important to me."

○

That night, I went to my senior's rooms, a bottle of sake and some deep-fried tofu in hand. As always, he was sitting in the center of his library, reading a book.

We seared the tofu using his electric heater, drizzled it with soy sauce, and ate it with the sake. My senior seemed to notice I wasn't my usual self, but he didn't say anything. I didn't plan to bring up the lies he'd heaped up over the months, figuring we could just go on as we had before. But I talked less than usual and drank recklessly. Before long, I was hammered.

The familiar forms of the bookshelf and the rounded back of my senior sitting across from me began to waver subtly, and I felt dizzy. He was withdrawn, too. He must have been as drunk as I was, because we both ended up lying between the stacks of books on the floor, groaning.

"Tell me a story."

"I'm not in the mood today."

"Oh, come on."

He stared silently at the ceiling for a few moments. "That reminds me, I guess Yuuki's moving to Tokyo soon," he finally said. "Another good-bye."

I didn't say anything, and eventually he started snoring.

I stood up and looked down at him as he slept. Curled up between the books with his arms wrapped around his body, he looked vulnerable.

I gripped my spinning head and threaded my way to the hallway, taking care not to knock over any books. It may have been spring, but the night air was still cold.

I opened the adjacent door and drank some water from the faucet at the kitchen sink.

As I was about to return to the library where my senior was sleeping, my gaze fell on the old bag lying next to his folded-up futon. It was the bag where he kept his sentimental possessions. The letters from his older brother, the pipe he'd bought at a bazaar, the short sword his father had brandished. That's what he'd told me.

I sat down on the tatami mat and gazed at the bag with unfocused eyes.

Then I reached out my hand and opened it.

○

When I got back to the library, my senior had vanished. Wondering where he could have gone in such a drunken state, I went outside. A train on the Eizan Electric Railway flashed past going north, leaving silence in its wake.

I wandered around searching for my senior in the glow of the streetlights. Eventually, I found myself at Lake Biwa Canal. A little concrete bridge spanned the water, with a vending machine on the far side. Its light threw into relief a cherry blossom tree in full bloom, making it look as if it had frozen white in the night air.

My senior was sitting beneath the cherry tree.

As I crossed the bridge and approached him, he suddenly looked up, then made as if he was trying to run away. He wasn't running from me, though. His gaze was fixed on something behind me. I turned around, but all I saw was the bridge lit up by a streetlight and the night road stretching away beyond it.

"You see that creature over there, don't you?" he said. "Look!"

I called out to him as I grabbed his shoulders, shaking them. "That's just something you made up."

"No, I didn't. It's there—right there."

"Those are all lies you made up," I said. "None of it exists."

Finally, as I stood there grasping his shoulders and staring at him, the tension in his body relaxed, and his face took on a vacant look. His shoulders slumped listlessly. I removed my hands and bought two cans of coffee from the vending machine next to him. Then we sat down under the cherry tree and drank them.

An Eizan Electric Railway train passed noisily south.

"How did you end up like this?" I asked.

He was quiet for a moment, then finally mumbled, "I'm not sure. It must have been that Silk Road journal."

"You really fooled me with that one."

"I found it near Nanzenji Temple. I read it over and over. It was just around the time I'd stopped going to class and shut myself up in my rooms, so I had more time than I knew what to do with… I could never go on a trip like that, so I admired the writer. Of course, it was the adventure of a total stranger."

"I really thought you'd traveled the Silk Road."

"I'm not that brave." He smiled bitterly and sipped his coffee. "Not too long after I read the journal, I was out in the city one day when I ran into a guy from that study group. I figured he would have forgotten me by then, since I hadn't attended a meeting in six months, but he remembered me. He was the friendly type, or should I say, the nosy type. He asked me what I'd been up to all those months I skipped out on the study group. In truth, I'd been holed up in my room doing nothing. But I couldn't say that. Almost reflexively, I said I'd gone on a trip."

"There are lots of university students who hole up in their rooms doing nothing, you know," I said.

"There probably are. But I couldn't say that. I felt embarrassed, or maybe disappointed in myself. I guess I thought that telling him the truth wouldn't do any good or that it would be like going backward."

"Still, that was one hell of a lie."

"The old me wouldn't have dreamed of saying something like that. Back then, I was always honest." He sighed deeply. "In the past, I was miserable at conversation. Whenever I tried to talk to someone, I had no idea what to say. I didn't know why it happened. I just knew I sounded like I was lying. I couldn't stand the hollow, false sound of my own voice. It only got worse after I started university, until I could hardly speak. I began to hate being around people and stopped leaving my room. I only survived because Yuuki stuck by me. If I hadn't met her in my first year of university, I would have been crushed."

"Are you telling the truth right now?" I blurted out.

"Who knows. What do you think? It could be a lie." He smiled. "You understand, don't you? In the past, I didn't have the composure to say what I'm saying right now. That's why I was always honest."

"I understand very well."

"When the guy from the study group came up to me on the street and I told that huge lie, I noticed something. I suddenly felt at ease. When I told him about the Silk Road trip, he loved it. He told me to come back to the study group. I did, and when I told some more lies, everyone thought they were great. People asked me why I'd gone on the trip, and I lied again. I made up stories about strange acquaintances, mysterious adventures, a fictitious family. As long as I was telling a lie, I was able to speak freely and shake off that sense that my words sounded false. That made me bolder. In other words, it became a compulsion."

He set his can on the ground and began stroking his fingers one by one.

"You know how I'm always writing? I'm working on a rough draft of my lies. A false autobiography from start to finish. I put a lot of careful preparation into telling good lies."

"You did an excellent job of it."

"The thing is, no matter how wonderful my lies are, they don't work without a good listener."

"Am I a good listener?"

"An ideal one. But not anymore, eh?"

"I wouldn't say that."

"You've found me out. It's all over now. I can't go to the study group anymore for the same reason. You probably didn't realize, but one of the guys there is bent on catching me in a lie."

He looked up at the cherry tree, its blossoms drifting through the night air.

"But you know, I still think to myself, *who cares if I'm lying?* I'm a boring, empty man. What value do I have aside from my stories?"

"Then why not go on telling lies?"

"Would you like to hear the next installment?"

"Of course."

And with that, my senior began his final story.

○

It was my last day of work at Hourendou.

I had ultimately decided to take off time from school and join my brother on his journey.

He planned to begin by following the Silk Road. Since it would likely be a long trip, I would have to quit my job at the curio shop. The owner was kind enough to be sad I was leaving and told me to visit again once I returned.

On my last day there, the curious American came in. The owner told him he'd found the magic lantern the man had been searching for. Apparently, it belonged to a client. Whether they would give it up or not depended on the offer, but the owner said he had arranged a viewing for him. I knew this was my only chance, so, at the risk of being pushy, I asked to come along. The owner made a call. That evening, he hung the CLOSED sign on the glass door, and the three of us set out to meet the client.

Our destination was an old mansion next to Saginomori Shrine at the top of a steep hill.

A strange feeling overtook me as I followed the owner up that hill. It was like I'd been there before. When I heard the bamboo rustling behind the grounds, I realized it was the mansion where I'd helped the book-loving baker make a delivery. That night, it had been dark, and I hadn't seen the place clearly, but the slope of the hill and the rustling of the bamboo grove behind the mansion were enough to assure me it was the same house.

We went into the garden, and the owner called out a greeting. A thin figure appeared on the veranda. They were wearing white Western-style clothes and a fox mask. I shrank back in surprise, but the figure took the mask off and smiled. I realized that what I had thought on my last visit was a man in a mask had in fact been a woman.

She seemed to be an old acquaintance of the owner, and although they exchanged few words, I could tell they knew each other well. No doubt the ease of their relationship was what prompted her to surprise us with the fox mask. The woman was young and said her name was Natsume. I thought it odd that she seemed to live alone in such a huge mansion.

We were led to an extremely long, narrow room. Other than a wall of translucent paper *shoji* facing a garden, the room was enclosed on three sides by sliding screens with strange pictures on them. One showed a dragon peeking between clouds. A creature with a long torso ran across another. On the last was an image of *torii* gates at an Inari shrine. We sat on a sofa and drank tea as we waited.

Dusk hung quietly over the garden.

Presently, Natsume returned and led us to an adjacent room.

This second room was large and empty. Closed off on all sides by opaque screens, it was pitch-black inside.

Natsume held a candle to each of the four corners. There, we saw what looked like film projectors made of paper, though I'd never seen anything like them before. Natsume then told us to sit down and placed a light in each of the contraptions. Each time she did so, the dimness of the room lessened slightly. A hazy image emerged in the center of the room and steadily came into focus.

Once she had finished lighting the magic lanterns, she came and sat beside us, her knees folded beneath her. The American let out a gasp of admiration. The owner remained silent. I held my breath.

A long, thin, sinuous beast had appeared in the center of the room. It was an odd creature, similar to a fox with an elongated body. Its round, fur-covered head was unlike that of a fox, however. The bared teeth and eyes it turned on us were somehow humanlike. The image of the beast flickered faintly along with the wavering candlelight, giving the impression it might begin to move at any moment.

"What is this animal?" the owner asked.

"I don't know why this kind of image was chosen for the lantern, but my father called it a lightning beast. He said he'd gotten it from a certain businessman."

As we gazed at it in admiration, Natsume smiled teasingly.

"Shall I show you something even more interesting?"

She stood up, walked over to the lamps, and blew them out. Then, using some trick, she ignited them again. A bluish light that rippled like the surface of a pool filled the room, and I instinctively rose on one knee. The magic lantern made the room look exactly as if it were flooded with water.

Natsume walked through the liquid, bluish-white light to the back of the room and pushed open a screen leading to another room behind it.

The smell of water rose to my nostrils, not an illusion this time.

Although the back room was dark, Natsume didn't light it. Instead, she slid farther into the darkness. A velvet curtain hung in the shadows. She silently pushed it open, and a bluish-white light gleamed out from the dark depths.

She turned toward us and beckoned, so I stepped through the blue light of the magic lanterns into the back room.

Beyond the curtain was an enormous tank of water, and coiled inside it, a huge serpentlike creature with shiny blue scales was visible. Its face, which reminded me of a crocodile's, rested on its scaly body. As I approached the tank, the eyes of this monster flashed suspiciously in my direction. I thought I saw its massive jaw move within the water, but it seemed to have grown weak, and it did not move its body.

No one said a word.

The creature had apparently been captured in the Meiji era, when the Lake Biwa Canal was being dug. Natsume told us that in the intervening century, it had changed hands several times before finally reaching her.

"One of these days, I plan to return it to where it came from."

Then she went to a chest of drawers in a corner of the room and took out a small, lacquered box. She reached in, pinched something between her thin fingers, and pulled it out: a netsuke of a dragon coiled inside a piece of fruit.

She placed this beautiful netsuke on my palm.

"This is for you," she said.

"Why?" I asked in surprise.

"To thank you." She smiled, then continued softly. "I remember the night you came here. You were the one who brought him, no?"

○

A few days later, a gift was delivered to my room.

When I returned from the university that evening, a paper bag and a card with my senior's name on it were waiting in my mailbox.

Inside the bag was the black-leather notebook containing my senior's autobiography and the dragon netsuke. There was no letter.

I rushed to his rooms, but they were deserted, all traces of his life there wiped clean. I wasn't surprised—I had expected this.

I left his building and walked toward Lake Biwa Canal.

Scattered clouds floated overhead, tinted pink by the evening sun. I followed the route I had taken the night I went looking for my senior and ended up at the little bridge spanning the canal. On the far side, the vending machine glowed brightly in the early dusk, lighting up the cherry tree beside it. That night, the tree had looked frozen in white, but in the space of a few short days, it had scattered the remainder of its blossoms, and green leaves could be seen sprouting up here and there on its branches.

I bought a can of coffee from the vending machine and smoked a cigarette as I gazed at the cherry petals scattered on the street.

I recalled what my senior had said to me as we parted.

"Sometimes I lose sight of the truth. My own scant experience is swallowed up by the lies I've created. I've never worked at a used bookstore or a curio shop, and I've never even been to Lake Biwa, let alone to the Silk Road. The antique-hunting American doesn't exist, and neither does the book-loving baker, or my autobiography-obsessed grandfather, or my street-performer brother, or the mysterious woman in the fox mask. But sometimes I recall them so vividly, it's like I remember them all for real. I feel like I might run into them when I'm out walking in the city."

I'm quite certain my senior believed he could create anything with his own hands. He shut himself up in his rooms and let his thoughts run over the sparkling lights of Kyoto and the dark corners where light doesn't reach, following the mysterious threads that dart in and out of view. Dazzled by his own creations, he glimpsed an enigmatic world. I believe this path of his, too, leads to a dark and mysterious place at the center of this city.

He said he was an empty, boring person.

But in all the time since he disappeared, I've never met anyone whose story is as worthy of retelling.

○

At the beginning of May, I went to Kyoto Station to see Mizuho off on her move to Tokyo. I made a point of going because I wanted to give her the netsuke I'd received from my senior. She had already been back and forth several times to move her things and fill out the necessary forms, and this was the day she finally planned to hand over the keys to her apartment.

The sky was perfectly blue, like it often is in May, and the air was clear and cool. Every corner of the city was bursting with fresh green leaves glistening with the previous day's rain.

I met Mizuho at a café in the station.

I told her my senior had disappeared, and I placed the netsuke on the table. But she shook her head. "You can have it," she said.

"I think you should take it. He did give it to you, after all."

"Actually, I was the one who gave it to him in the first place."

When Mizuho was a freshman in university, she worked weekends at a curio shop in Ichijoji called Hourendou. The shop's owner often went out or stayed in the back rooms, so Mizuho would sit in a narrow space between the tottering displays and idly pass the time.

At first, she was fascinated by the novelty of the curio trade and would wander around the shop looking at the old objects, wondering about their past. All sorts of things were set out with no apparent logic—dressers, a wooden statue of Budai, a huge copper frog, little lacquer boxes, fox masks, strange taxidermy animals, magic lanterns. But the same things were there every time she watched the shop, so gradually she grew bored of them. She would sit reading a novel and listen for the glass door to clatter open. Customers drifted in now and then, but the shop was hardly thriving.

Eventually, she noticed that a certain university student would often visit the shop. He would come every weekend and look silently at the curios. He didn't seem intent on buying anything. He just went around by himself, gazing at each object with a serious expression. She came to recognize him by the extremely intense look on his face.

One day, she talked to him.

He'd come in without a word, as usual, and was staring intensely at a little glass case full of netsuke and portable pillboxes. She happened to be tired of the book she was reading and feeling bored, so she walked over to him and asked if he'd like her to take anything out. He looked up in surprise and quietly said, "No." She peered into the glass case.

He stood there for a while without speaking before eventually pointing at one of the netsuke. It was a carving of a little dragon curled up inside a piece of fruit.

"Is that dragon inside a persimmon?" he asked.

Mizuho thought for a moment, then said, "Yes, it is."

"A persimmon, then."

"Yes, I think it's a persimmon."

"If it's a persimmon, then that dragon must be very small."

"Yes, very small."

She smiled, and he gave her a strange look.

After that, they talked often.

When the shop's owner was out and there weren't any other customers, the two of them would share long conversations. Sometimes he brought sake lees, and they toasted them over the heater. He didn't talk much, but she could tell he chose his words carefully. She thought of his words like raindrops dripping down from the eaves, eventually making a soft hollow in the ground below. She felt he was an honest person.

Eventually, Mizuho told him she was going to quit her job at Hourendou. "That's a pity," he said. He didn't say anything else. On her final day, when she was getting ready to go home, the shop's owner said, "If there's anything you'd like, I'll sell it to you for cheap." She thought about it for a moment, then asked for the dragon netsuke he'd said he couldn't afford.

She gave it to him as a gift.

"Come to think of it, neither of you ever told me how you met."

"It felt embarrassing to bring up."

"Is that all?"

Mizuho picked up the dragon netsuke and stared at it.

"Do you think he really forgot I gave this to him?"

"I think it's possible."

"That's a very mean thing to say so casually."

"I'm a man who cannot lie."

"Liar."

Her train was coming soon, so we headed to the platform.

The bullet train came sliding in, and she picked up her shoulder bag. Just before she stepped on, I glimpsed a shadow of sadness flicker over her face, which until then had showed only relief. But perhaps it was my imagination. She didn't say anything unnecessary.

She took my hand and pressed the dragon netsuke into my palm. I tried to give it back, but she stopped me.

"Well, good-bye."

"Good-bye."

I raised my hand, still grasping the netsuke.

Even after the train left Kyoto Station, I kept standing, looking vacantly down the tracks.

Eventually, I started walking across the bright, empty platform.

Phantom

I loved the feeling of an approaching downpour. Dark clouds would lope across the summer sky like huge beasts, plunging the dry city streets into shadow, and the air would fill with a sweet smell like fruit. The first drop had yet to fall. When I walked through the city at such moments, I felt as if my body was shivering with excitement.

I saw her for the first time in the rain, and I met her for the last time in the rain as well.

Large drops were pelting down from the sky so hard that they hurt, bouncing off the asphalt in a hazy spray. I remember the moment blue lightning illuminated her drenched form, the wooden sword in her hand glistening.

○

Nishida Spirits was located down a maze of backstreets, with the lush foliage of the Imperial Garden looming just to the west.

I went there for the first time in May. The map my friend had drawn for me was wrong, and I ended up walking up and down the narrow alleys looking for the shop. A cool breeze was blowing down the streets, and the sky as it turned from pink to indigo was beautiful.

On one corner, there was a little smoke shop. The light from the row of vending machines next to it lit up the whole alley. I peered into the dim shop and saw a little old lady sitting with a blanket over her knees, half buried in junk. I bought a pack of cigarettes and asked her where Nishida Spirits was.

Following her directions, I soon found the store.

The shutters were up, and light was spilling onto the street. Cases of beer and cardboard boxes were piled on the pavement. From inside the half-open glass doors, I could hear raucous chatter. I stood outside hesitating, unable to find the right moment to go in. Eventually, a middle-aged man with a hand towel twisted around his forehead came outside and reached for one of the cardboard boxes, muttering to himself. "Excuse me," I said.

He turned toward me, loudly asking, "What?" His eyebrows were thick and black, but the beard that covered his cheeks and jaw was flecked with white.

"Um, about the tutor...," I began, but before I could finish, his face brightened and he interrupted with an "aha!"

Then he turned toward the store and called out in his booming voice, "Heeey!"

A friend from university had told me about the job at Nishida Spirits.

The work entailed tutoring the younger of the owner's two sons, who was about to start high school. My friend had started as an assistant at the liquor store but had quickly insinuated himself into a position as the family's tutor.

This predecessor of mine had maneuvered to boost my

reputation with the Nishida family even before I met them, which was why they welcomed me so warmly from the start. The pay wasn't that high, but I didn't have an agency taking a cut, and the family often invited me for dinner or drinks, so I had nothing to complain about.

The truth is, I used to get drunk with my student's father on a regular basis. Around nine at night, he'd come creaking up the old staircase to the second-floor room where I tutored his son. He wasn't coming to check on his son's studies but instead to invite me to drink. After a while, I had hit it off so well with him, and felt so comfortable downstairs, I wasn't sure if I was there to tutor or to drink.

Since my student's father had invited me to these drinking parties himself, I tended to get carried away, and this would cause his wife to become increasingly testy and occasionally scold me. However, she always scolded me through her husband, never to my face. "I think that's enough now," she would call out to him, fed up, from the back room where she was doing some task or another. I would abruptly stop my boisterous laughter, set down my cup of sake, and meekly shut my mouth.

Each time she blew up like that, the two of us would lay low for a little while.

○

The Nishida family lived in a two-story wooden building next to the liquor store. You could enter either from a gate facing onto the street or from the concrete entryway of the liquor store, which was connected to the living room. Sometimes I went in through the store and chatted with one of my student's parents before going into the house, but when there were customers in the shop, I went in through the proper entryway.

I would push open the sliding screen door and call out my greeting, and as I was taking off my shoes, my student would come about halfway down the stairs and answer, "Hey." As I followed him back up the creaking staircase, I'd ask, "Ready?" and he'd reply with a lackluster "guess so."

My student's name was Shuuji. My first impression was that he was an absentminded, hard-to-pin-down type. Until we got used to each other, we never talked about anything besides his studies. But sharing drinks with his father solidified my position, and eventually the tension between us relaxed.

Shuuji was quite a bit larger than I was. He had a thick chest, and you could see his well-toned muscles through his clothes. As I sat beside him, watching his large back curl over his desk, I felt as if a hard, beautifully crafted sheet of steel were being made to bend, and I felt sorry for him. He didn't seem to pay much attention to his looks, and I remember the waves of his short hair would be raging in some new direction each time we met.

Before long, as I got used to him and began to understand the quiet emotions rippling in the depths of his heart, I came to like this laconic high school student.

I even used to stop at the neighborhood snack shop to buy his favorite food, Nishimura Health Biscuits, and we'd crunch on them between study sessions. He would chuckle happily as I placed the little round biscuits in his big palm, swallowing them in one gulp. His impressive, broad-shouldered build reminded me of his father, who looked like the product of nomadic stock, but Shuuji's face was like his mother's, and when he smiled, he had a cuteness that could have come only from her.

"I never get sick of these things," he said.

"You have some weird taste," I said, pinching a health biscuit between my fingers.

○

An unsettling wind had been blowing since morning. All day, clouds had hung heavy over the city, but the rain seemed like it would never come. As I walked down the dim staircase of my apartment building, a lukewarm breeze blew up it, brushing my cheeks. I'd been lazy about picking up my newspapers, so my mailbox was stuffed full.

Raindrops started to plop down as I crossed Kojin Bridge. I rested my hands on the railing and looked north. The mountains in the distance were hazy. The wind was blowing my hair in all directions. I knew I needed to get to Nishida Spirits before the rain got worse, but I also wanted to take my time and wander around under the unsettled sky.

I liked exploring the tangled backstreets, so every time I went to my tutoring job, I took a different route. Even the smallest neighborhood revealed a different face on each visit, making me want to head down every narrow side alley I came upon. I often left my apartment early and strolled around the neighborhood on my way to Nishida Spirits, paying no mind to the length of my route.

When dusk began to fall, the side alleys grew more mysterious. They were nostalgic and eerie at the same time. Walking down them, I felt as if I might get lost and never find my way out. I used to wonder if something was lying in wait for me at the end of one of their branches. Just before the rain, that sense would grow even stronger.

One day, I crossed Kojin Bridge and walked north down a narrow street.

Among the cafés and apartment buildings lining my path was a two-story wooden shop. Its old, carved wooden sign read NATSUODOU. Dusk was falling earlier than usual because of the thick, low clouds, and the shop lights twinkled in the evening shadows. Through the glass doors, I could see bamboo swords propped against a wall, so I knew right away it was a martial arts equipment shop.

In the distance, I heard thunder rumbling like the rolling of an enormous wheel.

A girl wearing a high school uniform came walking toward me.

Just as I reached the Natsuodou storefront, the rain began to pitter-patter. The girl skipped lightly in my direction and then, in a fluid motion, twirled around to grab hold of the glass door. Her short, blunt-cut black hair gleamed in the light of the shop.

Shrieking, she slipped in through the gap between the doors.

As the sound of the rain enveloped me, I opened my umbrella and continued past the shop. The girl pressed her face against the glass and peered at the clouds. I glanced inside, and her eyes met mine. She pulled her face back, frowning at me ever so slightly.

○

Shuuji told me he'd first picked up a bamboo sword the year he started elementary school. He joined a dojo called Seifuukan with his brother, Naoya, who was a year older. His teacher, Takeda-sensei, was the owner of the dojo and an acquaintance of his father's, which was why the man had pushed his two boys into joining. According to Shuuji, not many elementary students were enrolling in the dojo these days, but back when he and his brother started, there had been lots of kids their age.

"Everyone started to quit when they reached junior high. The only ones who still show up are my brother, Akizuki, and me. Even Natsuo quit in junior high."

"Do you and Naoya go to the dojo a lot?"

"No, we're too busy with kendo club at school to go that often. But if we don't stop by now and then, Takeda-sensei gets mad."

I could imagine that learning kendo with his brother must have sparked a rivalry between them. When I asked who was the better fighter, he answered without hesitation. "Oh, my brother's better. I'm no match for him."

"Aren't you bigger?"

"That's not the only thing that matters."

"That so?"

"Yeah. My brother's really good. But Natsuo used to be even better than him."

If Shuuji's brother was good, then I imagined Natsuo must be some brawny giant of a guy. But when I said this to Shuuji, he burst out laughing.

That was the first time I heard Mika Natsuo's name.

She was the daughter of the family who owned the martial arts equipment store Shuuji and Naoya frequented, and she had started at Seifuukan even before they had. She was the same age as Naoya, which made her a year older than Shuuji. From elementary school through the end of junior high, she'd been the star of both the school kendo club and of Seifuukan. When Shuuji talked about her accomplishments, he looked as proud as if he was talking about himself.

But in the summer of her third year of junior high, she'd left

Seifuukan and quit the junior high kendo club. Abruptly, she had severed all connections with kendo.

○

I could never find a chance to talk to Shuuji's brother, Naoya. He either stayed late at school practicing kendo or went to Seifuukan to teach the younger kids. He was a quiet boy, and even when he was in the house, I never realized he was there.

Before I managed to talk to Naoya, I met Akizuki.

One day, when I walked into Shuuji's room, a skinny kid with glasses was sitting cross-legged on the cushion I usually sat on, reading books. Despite the steamy heat, he was slurping a big bowl of ramen. His face beaded with sweat and noodles hanging from his mouth, he was chatting with Shuuji, who was at work at his desk. When I walked in, the newcomer bowed his head, sending his neatly trimmed bangs swinging. He looked comical and sensitive at the same time.

"That moron over there is Akizuki," Shuuji informed me.

"Shut up," Akizuki replied, turning toward me. "Bet you've got a hard job," he said, his voice full of pity. "There's not much point in teaching this guy. He's an idiot."

"But he gets paid for it," Shuuji pointed out

"Still sounds like a waste of time."

"Look who's talking."

Shuuji spun his chair around and pretended to kick Akizuki, but he nimbly dodged the blow.

"I'm gonna get you, and I'm not coming to your funeral, either."

"Like I'd want you there!"

After they'd trash-talked each other for a while, Akizuki said loudly, "I can't believe Naoya isn't back yet!" then left the room. I could hear him clomping down the stairs before shouting, "Hey, Auntie, I'm leaving my bowl over here!" He was acting as cocky and noisy as if he was in his own home.

Apparently, he'd made plans with Naoya to go to Seifuukan that evening, but Naoya was late coming back from school. Akizuki had gotten bored of waiting and asked Shuuji's mom to make him some ramen, then wolfed it down next to Shuuji while the latter slaved over his homework.

Akizuki was the son of the priest at the local temple.

I'd followed its long wall a few times on my walks. It was quite impressive.

Akizuki had started out at Seifuukan and had belonged to the same high school club as Shuuji and Naoya, but I'd heard he was expelled for getting in too many fights. The reason he showed up so often at Seifuukan was that he couldn't do kendo at school anymore.

His penchant for fighting dated back to the end of junior high. He didn't fight at school but out in the city. He'd go for a stroll in a downtown neighborhood like Shinkyogoku and right away get into it with someone. Shuuji said he probably walked around looking like he was itching for a fight. He was just average at kendo, but when it came to street fights, he was so fast that he'd get in two or three punches to his opponent's face before they even knew what was happening. Then, while the other guy was still groaning, he'd run off.

"It's the one thing he's good at," Shuuji said. "I'll give him that."

"I'd never guess it from his looks," I said.

"He hasn't been doing it lately."

"Think he got bored of it?"

"Well, a lot of stuff happened."

Shuuji stared absently out the window, like he was deep in thought.

○

As I walked down an alley hemmed in on both sides by wooden fences, I had a mounting sense that something was lying in wait for me farther back. I ventured into an overgrown lot off the alley, and the feeling reached a peak. The flitting of insects should have been the only movement around me, but I had the feeling that something was creeping slowly my way from the back of the lot, ready to leap.

The grass was thick and tall and the hot air stagnant. I could see a ramshackle house on the other side of the lot and realized I must be in its garden. Aside from a narrow lane leading to the street, the entire property was surrounded by a wall, cutting it off from the outside world. Since there was no nameplate at the entrance to the lane, I had assumed it led through to another street and was surprised to find it didn't.

According to Shuuji's mother, the abandoned house had once been owned by a family who ran two or three restaurants. When their business went bust, they'd skipped town. A person claiming to be a relative of the former owners had come to see the property once, but after that, there had been no more visitors, and it was left to disintegrate. Apparently, all sorts of weird rumors had been lingering around the place for years. Though it was supposed to be abandoned, Shuuji's mother said people claimed to see lights on at night or hear beast-like howls.

On the trunk of a low tree in the garden, a cicada chirped loudly.

I could see the house's veranda, but the shutters were closed tight. What looked like a little shrine was buried in grass, along with a well. All that was left of the well was a square enclosure made of piled stones with a corrugated sheet on top.

The brightness of the sun somehow made my surroundings seem even darker. The shadows cast by the trees were disturbingly deep. There was a sweet smell like something rotting—similar, too, to the smell just before a downpour. The cicada that had been chirping so relentlessly suddenly stopped, and the garden went silent.

I gasped.

I wasn't sure if it had appeared without my noticing or had been lurking there all along, but next to the old well was a creature resembling a fox. Unlike a fox, however, its trunk was unsettlingly long. Its face was round, not pointed. And the eyes, which stared at me intently, looked more human than beast-like.

Was it this creature I'd sensed? I wondered to myself.

For some reason, I felt afraid to look away, so I stood there, unable to move, as if possessed. But staring into its eyes was no less terrifying. Time crawled, slow as oil. I felt sweat dripping from my temples down my cheeks.

Suddenly, the creature bared a set of white, humanlike teeth and made a motion as if it was about to leap at me.

○

July arrived.

The rainy season was still in full swing, and most days, the sky was covered in unbroken clouds. I had to cross the swollen Kamo River to get to Nishida Spirits. Walking over the Kojin Bridge,

I would look down at the rushing, muddy water. I often gazed absently at the yellowish froth appearing and disappearing on the water's surface. The cityscape far downstream always looked hazy.

Starting in mid-June, I'd been turning the screws on Shuuji in preparation for his final exams, and at last the cruel final stretch had ended.

"Did your work pay off?" I asked him.

"If I failed at this point, I really would be hopeless."

"If you can say that, you're in good shape."

"By the way, you haven't been looking so good lately."

"I don't like the rainy season."

"It's really coming down this year. It's gotta end soon, though." Shuuji's face brightened. "It's finally summer vacation."

Since starting university, time had begun to feel formless to me, like the hazy rainy-season sky, but for Shuuji, it was still sharply divided into segments. Even though he'd just be practicing kendo all day every day, he was looking forward to his break from school after the end-of-semester ceremony.

That night, I assigned Shuuji some arbitrary homework, and then, for the first time in a while, I had some drinks with his father.

Outside, the rain seemed to be pouring down ceaselessly in the dark. If I listened closely, I could hear the drops plopping down onto the leaves of the aralia planted outside the window. I imagined the wet, palm-shaped leaves glistening moistly in the darkness. Shuuji's father was unusually quiet and humorless.

"The Yoiyama festival's coming up. Are you going?" he asked abruptly.

Yoiyama took place the night before the big Gion parade. I'd been once, at the invitation of a friend. All I could remember was being unable to move in the crush of people. Trapped within the pushing, shoving crowd, I'd felt like I couldn't breathe—hardly the right state for enjoying a night festival.

"No, I don't plan to."

"No?"

Having lost his conversational thread, he fell silent again. I tried to make up for it by starting a new topic, but I seemed to have lost my touch. I slipped into a daze listening to the rain outside the window.

"Be careful on your way home," Shuuji's father said.

"Why do you say that?"

"Lately people have been getting attacked on the street at night. We've been talking about setting up a neighborhood patrol."

"Think it's a robber?"

"No, nothing like that. The criminal has been ambushing people with some kind of blunt object and then running off."

This seemed to be the reason he had been so uncharacteristically pensive that evening. I'd heard from Shuuji that his dad called the shots in the crime-prevention committee of the neighborhood association.

"I'll watch out." I smiled and swallowed my sake. Shuuji's father gave me a hard look.

"This is no joke. Some people have been seriously hurt. You really need to be careful. If you see anyone suspicious on the street, get out of there fast."

○

I started leaving earlier for Nishida Spirits. It's not that I was spending more time teaching Shuuji math or English but that my habit of exploring the neighborhood on the way had begun to intensify.

In the wake of the rainy season, blinding sunshine brought out the charm of the city in midsummer. When I crossed the bridge, I often saw people cooling their feet in the sparkling water of the Kamo River. My surroundings began to look more and more like an illusion. However far I ventured down the alleyways, they were jammed full of a stuffy heat that made my mind grow fuzzy as I pushed through it.

Summer vacation had begun.

One afternoon, as I walked through a backstreet hazy with heat, I came to the smoke shop where I had asked for directions on my first visit. The strong sunlight illuminating the street made the inside of the shop look even darker. Wiping away my sweat, I stepped under the eaves and peered into the store. As I did so, I heard a sound like a monkey's screech coming from the dusky shop. This was followed by the sound of someone making their way between the mountains of junk. I glimpsed something small practically somersaulting toward the back of the shop. After that, all was silent.

"Excuse me!" I shouted. No one replied.

Toward the back of the smoke shop was a small, half-open sliding door, and through that I could see a hallway with a wood floor. A small steel fan was pushing the muggy air around, and the television in the corner had been left on.

After a few moments, a young woman with her hair in a ponytail pushed open the door. She gave me a slightly wary look, so I bowed my head and asked for some cigarettes. "Oh, of course, I'm sorry," she said, taking a pack out for me.

"Is someone back there?" I asked, pointing to the sliding door in the back. An apologetic look came over her face.

"My mother. Lately she's scared of everything. I don't know what to do."

"I didn't mean to surprise her."

"It's not your fault. This is the third time it's happened."

I bought a cola from the vending machines outside and drank it. My eyes teared up from the prickly sensation on my throat, but I was so sweaty, it tasted good. As I rested, hunched in the sliver of shade under the shop's eaves, the woman came out and tidied up for a few minutes, then asked, "Are you a university student?"

"Yeah," I answered, lighting a cigarette.

"Do you live around here?"

"No. I'm a tutor for the family who runs the liquor store."

"Oh, for the Nishidas?"

We started chatting, and the topic of the night attacks came up. She said five people had already been ambushed. The victims had been walking the alleys at night when it happened. None of them had seen the attacker's face. No sooner did they notice something slipping past them than a hard blow fell, and everything went white. The victims were scattered among three nearby neighborhoods, and their neighborhood associations were cooperating to patrol the area.

The woman said her mother didn't believe the attacker was human, then laughed cynically, dismissing the idea as an elderly person's overactive imagination. Still, as she talked, her face tensed slightly.

"She says it's the work of a phantom passing through."

"What do you mean, a phantom?"

"Who knows? Something like a spirit, I guess." She tilted her head and shrugged. "It's really inconvenient not being able to go out at night. The worst thing is how much it scares the children and the elderly." She lowered her voice. "My mother is in the back right now. She said your face when you peered in the window looked like the face of some big creature."

"Like a phantom?"

"It's awful, isn't it? I'm sorry," she said, frowning.

○

"We'll walk you partway home," Shuuji called as I was about to leave Nishida Spirits. It was just after eleven at night. Naoya was coming down the stairs behind him. The sight of these two massive brothers pulling their shoelaces tight in the entryway was quite imposing.

"Isn't this a bit much?" I asked.

"Nah. We're doing the rounds tonight. Dad's at the fire brigade office."

As the three of us emerged into the dark street, the hot night air hit my cheeks. Now and then, a cool breeze blew past, but the asphalt hadn't yet lost the heat of the day. The neighborhood had sunk into nighttime shadow. Other than the sound of cars passing on the main street, all I could hear was our footsteps. Shuuji said the neighborhood was quieter than usual because of the recent attacks. Streetlights shone down on us at regular intervals. In their momentary light, I glanced at the two boys walking next to me. Shuuji's expression was relaxed, but Naoya looked tense.

"Has practice been tough?" I asked.

"The usual. Sometimes I feel like I'm gonna die," Shuuji said, laughing. "That's why I can't go to the dojo very often, and Takeda-sensei gets so mad."

"That's rough."

"You should come to the dojo sometime," Shuuji said, glancing at Naoya. Naoya nodded.

"We're doing a watermelon meetup soon—how about coming to that?" he offered.

"What's a watermelon meetup?"

"We eat watermelon grown by Takeda-sensei's friend..."

"In that case, I'll try to make it."

"Akizuki's coming, too. And probably Natsuo. Maybe. Right?"

"Yeah, everyone usually comes."

We came to a house with an orange light glowing behind lattice doors. A poster advertising the schedule for an upcoming series of *kyogen* performances was taped to the front of them. Shuuji was talking about watermelons, but Naoya seemed to be frowning slightly in the orange light. His gaze was fixed on the dark street corner ahead of us.

"See that?" he whispered sharply.

Shuuji stopped talking, and the three of us looked down the street. It stretched to the south, lined on both sides with houses, until it formed a T with the wall of the temple where Koujun Akizuki lived. A slender human form was moving back and forth near the wall. I was staring at it, suddenly nervous, when Shuuji said in a deflated voice, "Oh, geez. I think it's Natsuo."

The figure remained in front of the wall until we drew near. At some point, she seemed to notice us, because she turned in our direction and stopped moving. Her white face glowed in the light of the streetlamp. "Hello," she said to the two brothers before giving me a suspicious look. She didn't seem to remember our encounter in front of Natsuodou.

"This is my tutor," Shuuji said. I bowed my head, and so did she.

"What are you doing out here?" Naoya scolded. "It's dangerous; you shouldn't be walking around at night."

"Sorry," Natsuo said, but she didn't seem too bothered. She said she was bringing snacks for the night patrol and held up a plastic bag to show us.

"What's that?" Shuuji asked.

"Rice balls," she replied.

Farther down the temple wall and off to the west a little was a small building that belonged to the fire brigade.

The door facing the street was open, and bright light spilled out. We could hear loud conversation coming from inside, and the drunken voice of Shuuji and Naoya's father was the loudest of all. "You came down, too, huh?" Naoya asked, peering in.

"Sure did," Akizuki answered brightly. The gathering felt more like a fun summer festival than a serious patrol. I didn't want to bother with properly greeting all the members of the neighborhood association, so I stood in the dark outside and listened in on their conversations.

That was where I parted ways with Shuuji and Naoya.

"Be careful out there," Shuuji said. "Looking forward to that watermelon. You coming to that, Natsuo?"

"To the watermelon meetup? Sure am."

She nodded at Shuuji, then turned to me, seeming perplexed.

○

After splitting up with Shuuji and Naoya, I pressed on through the dark neighborhood. A big red moon glimmered through the rifts in the gray clouds, throwing them into high relief. I felt as if a huge animal were looking down on me from behind the clouds.

Instead of heading straight for Kojin Bridge, I took a slightly roundabout route.

I turned down a long, straight street. On the right was a house with a brick wall outside, and when I looked in through the iron lattice gate halfway down the wall, I saw a lamp glowing under the eaves on the far side of the garden. On the left side of the street was the high wall of a high school. The old concrete was dingy from wind and rain and covered in stains that resembled a sort of design. The building on the other side was dark and looked abandoned.

I walked on, trailing my blurred and scattered shadow.

Far down the street, at the break in another brick wall, several vending machines were bursting with light and scattering it all around. They stood in front of a shuttered shop covered in posters that had been left to bleed in the rain, the business long since shut down.

I bought a can of juice.

The can let out a sigh as I opened it, deepening the silence of my surroundings. Hemmed in by brick and concrete walls, the arrow-straight street felt like just the sort of place the smoke shop woman's phantom might race through.

As I drank my juice and gazed at the wall around the high school, the shadow of a fox-like creature rushed nimbly along the top of it.

○

The Seifuukan dojo was near Goryo Shrine. To the left was a public bathhouse, and to the right was a row of houses. It was evening when I visited, and I spotted a skinny old man, a wash basin full of bath things sandwiched under his arm, slip through the curtain at the entrance to the bathhouse. The street-side door to the dojo was open, and I could hear children shouting inside. On the wall next to the door was a poster reading, NEW SWORDSMEN WANTED.

The building was made of time-burnished wood. When I walked in through the sliding doors, I found the entire concrete entryway scattered with little shoes. Just beyond them was an elevated wooden floor. As I peered inside, Shuuji came walking over. "We're going to eat the watermelon after we finish cleaning," he said. He looked handsome in his navy kendo outfit.

Naoya was standing in the room behind him, and at his command, a line of about ten elementary school children bent down in unison and began polishing the floor with cloths. They advanced toward me, laughing loudly, like they were racing one another. When they reached my feet, they spun around and returned in the opposite direction, wiping the floor again. I couldn't help smiling at the sight of their round bottoms, wrapped in long navy *hakama*, wiggling away from me.

"Lively place," I said.

"Used to be livelier," Shuuji replied.

"Aren't there any junior high students?"

"A couple practice here, but they're not around today."

Having finished the floor, the kids were now swinging their rags around at one another.

I took my shoes with me and followed Shuuji to a door on one side of the dojo that led outside. Then we passed down a narrow lane to the back of the building.

We emerged into a small yard that smelled of grass, enclosed by concrete walls. Dozens of small towels were hanging from a dirty clothesline, the white cotton patterned with navy. There was an old stone well, and next to it stood Natsuo and a short, robust middle-aged man. At their feet was a large basin of water with three watermelons floating in it, the mere sight of which refreshed me. Natsuo looked my way, scratching a mosquito bite on her arm.

"Thanks for having me today," I said, bowing my head. The middle-aged man inclined his thick chest a few degrees without speaking.

Takeda-sensei was built very much like Shuuji's father. His thick eyebrows and clear-cut features were similar as well, but unlike Shuuji's father, Takeda-sensei was so handsome, it was almost too much, and his beautifully shaped head was completely bald.

"That's a nice old well," I said. "Do you still use it?"

"If you don't use a well every day, it'll go bad," he said. Then he fell silent again. He didn't even look at me.

"Let's get started," Naoya said, emerging from the dojo.

He and Natsuo set up a folding table in the street out front and sliced into the watermelons. As soon as they'd cut a batch of misshapen pieces, the kids grabbed them. They ate noisily, sitting or standing around the table.

"Here you go," Shuuji said, handing me a huge slice.

It wasn't that sweet, but I gulped down the juicy flesh, and it soothed my throat, which was dry from the heat. Breathing in the watery smell, I looked up at the sky. Beyond the blue roof tiles of the neighboring houses, thunderheads tinted pink and orange by the sunset rose so high, they seemed about to pierce the heavens. I felt like a child on summer vacation again.

Shuuji constantly had a group of kids hanging around him. They didn't seem as keen on Naoya, Takeda-sensei, or Natsuo, but they clung instinctively to Shuuji.

Eventually, Akizuki arrived on his bicycle, and the kids got even more excited.

After leaning his bicycle in front of the dojo, Akizuki immediately bit into a slice of watermelon. When the kids swarmed around him, he began shooting seeds out of his mouth like bullets and chasing the squealing children. Finally, he caught one of the boys by the back of his collar and spit a mouthful of seeds down his uniform. The boy shrieked. Natsuo, who had been standing with Takeda-sensei and Naoya, strode over and yelled at him to get a handle on himself but retreated when he spit seeds on her.

"What a moron," Shuuji mumbled.

The dusky alley was as lively as a festival night. The neighbors seemed to be aware of the event, and I saw a couple of people walking their dog or returning from the store stop to chat with Takeda-sensei.

"You seem popular with the kids," I said to Shuuji.

"Guess so," he said, smiling wryly. "I've been keeping an eye on them since they started here."

"It's hard to imagine you being that small once," I said, looking at the kids. Shuuji nodded, taking a bite of watermelon.

"I was. We all were—my brother, Akizuki, and Natsuo."

○

As the evening light faded, the kids began to disperse and head home. Eventually, the high school students, Takeda-sensei, and I were the only ones left. Just as I was thinking of leaving, Akizuki and Naoya started talking about having a match.

I sat down cross-legged by the wall of the dojo and watched the two of them put on their gear. Shuuji and Natsuo were talking quietly beside me, but I couldn't hear what they were saying. Takeda-sensei switched on the fluorescent lights, and the dojo took on a lonely, washed-out atmosphere.

When the match began, Akizuki let out a sound like some kind of eerie bird, which surprised me. Naoya's call was lower in pitch, like he was scooping the sound up from inside himself. Each time one of them landed a hit, the floor shook, jolting me where I sat in the corner. Very quickly, I could tell that Akizuki was at a disadvantage. Compared to Naoya, whose stance remained solid no matter how many times they clashed, Akizuki was stumbling more and more.

Akizuki lunged at Naoya, but the instant before they crashed, Naoya leaped back and swung his bamboo sword. Naoya shouted, "Iiei!" and Takeda-sensei raised a hand slightly in his direction. Akizuki spun away from Naoya, dropping his hands listlessly to his sides.

"Was that the end?" I whispered to Shuuji.

"Yeah."

They faced off a second time, but while Naoya's body seemed to have become lighter, Akizuki looked as if he was burdened by a heavy weight. Akizuki landed a blow on Naoya's mask, but Takeda-sensei didn't raise his hand. Akizuki's long, drawn-out "eeeeeeeeehn" reverberated, sounding hollow. He repositioned his sword and twisted his neck.

"Akizuki has a lot of bad habits," Shuuji said. "He's never listened to Takeda-sensei."

"There's not much you can do with that kind of unnecessary baggage," Natsuo muttered.

The floor shook dramatically, and Naoya's husky voice rang out.

He landed a blow on Akizuki's mask, ending the fight.

○

In August, there was a string of peaceful nights. I heard that Shuuji's father was spearheading an effort to reform the patrols, which had grown lax. Before he managed to do so, however, there was an incident.

Several men had gathered at a shop in Marutamachi to play mah-jongg, and as they were strolling home, they spotted a suspicious character. It was a young, lanky man carrying a long stick. Partly because they were drunk, the men assumed it was the phantom attacker and lost their cool. Without pausing to think, they leaped on him, dragging him out of the shadows beyond the reach of the streetlights, only to discover the suspicious youth was Akizuki.

They brought him straight to the fire brigade office, but the boy insisted he'd simply been patrolling the neighborhood. He'd been carrying his bamboo sword, which he said he needed in case he was ambushed by the phantom attacker. Although they'd dragged him to the office, the men knew him and felt uncomfortable interrogating him too harshly. Unsure what to do, they waited for the president of the neighborhood association, Mr. Nishida, and Akizuki's father, the priest, to arrive.

All three rushed to the office, but Akizuki continued to claim he had been falsely accused.

Finally, Naoya walked in, a calm expression on his face. He was carrying his bamboo sword as well. He explained the situation, clearing Akizuki of suspicion. Since the night patrols had grown lax, the two of them had been trying to catch the criminal themselves, he said. They were told not to interfere without permission, and the incident came to an end. For the time being, Akizuki's good name was restored.

However, word that he had been the target of suspicion soon spread around the neighborhood.

As it did, people began talking about reinstating the charges he had initially been cleared of. “My dad doesn't trust him, either,” Shuuji said. For the time being, Akizuki's father forbid him from leaving the temple grounds, and I heard he sat moping on the veranda of the main shrine from morning till night.

○

The wind was blowing the rain around, and the sound of the storm outside the window kept receding and approaching. The moment I thought the rain had eased, it would start pouring down again. A tepid breeze blew in through the window screen.

A week had passed since Akizuki was confined to the temple grounds. In the interval, no new attacks had occurred.

I looked out the window. The tile roof across the alley looked dismal. The whole sky was ashen, with no break in the clouds. I imagined Akizuki sitting cross-legged in the humid temple. Shuuji and Naoya were worried about him, but I suspected that in the eye of the storm, Akizuki was probably yawning with boredom and stuffing his face with sweet-bean buns or something.

“Want to take a break?” I asked. Shuuji nodded.

We slouched against the wall side by side, ate some puffed rice, and drank some tea. For a while, we were both silent. “Wonder why my brother didn't ask me to go with them,” Shuuji said. “I could have gone around with Akizuki and kept him out of trouble.”

“Why doesn't anyone believe him? Naoya explained what they were doing, right?”

"Yeah, but there are some things about Akizuki that just raise people's suspicions."

"Like how he gets in fights?"

"Not just that."

Shuuji seemed to be considering whether or not to tell me more. I decided not to push him. I could hear the rain beating down and Shuuji's father talking to a customer downstairs. Finally, Shuuji started telling me the story of why Akizuki had quit the kendo club.

It had happened before Shuuji started high school.

In the past, the kendo club that Naoya and Shuuji belonged to had several mean, older members who made trouble about every little thing. They had harassed Akizuki and Naoya pretty badly when they joined the club as freshmen. Although Naoya was a quiet boy, he confronted problems head-on when he had to, and Akizuki wasn't the type to silently endure, either. A series of fights broke out in the club, and they could no longer even hold practice. Eventually, Naoya rounded up some sympathetic club members and tried to force the problematic seniors to quit the club.

Needless to say, the older members weren't about to take this silently and cooked up their own scheme to bully Naoya into silence. One night, they attacked him on the street. As a result, he was injured and couldn't practice kendo for some time. According to Shuuji, Akizuki took revenge into his own hands. He targeted each of the older students when they were out alone at night, attacking them one by one. It was hard to deny his methods were similar to those of the phantom attacker.

"That's why he had to leave the kendo club and why people don't trust him."

"Did the students who were forced to quit stay quiet after that?"

"Sometime later, Akizuki was attacked on the street at night. They beat him to a pulp."

"I guess that figures."

"Akizuki wouldn't say who attacked him. He changed a little after that. Stopped getting into fights."

Shuuji turned back to his assignment.

As I stepped out of the room after our session, I saw Natsuo climbing the stairs. Her slightly disheveled hair was flecked with water droplets. When she saw me, she frowned for a second, then quickly smiled.

"How's Shuuji doing on his lessons?"

"The future is bleak," I said, looking her in the eye.

She went into Naoya's room. As she closed the sliding door from inside, I glimpsed her eyes through the crack. I felt her gaze pierce me like an arrow.

○

In order to cheer up the falsely accused Akizuki in his temple prison, Shuuji suggested lighting some fireworks. Since using fire on the wooden veranda was prohibited, the group of childhood friends planned to gather at the temple gate and set off rainbow-colored sparklers on the sidewalk. I imagined the street filled with white smoke and the smell of gunpowder as countless points of light exploded, then disappeared.

When Shuuji invited me, I had agreed to join them. But as twilight fell, I started to feel increasingly gloomy and didn't want to cross Kojin Bridge. I called Shuuji and canceled, telling him something had come up. I didn't feel like going anywhere else, and I simply sat in my room as the light faded.

After the sun set, I went out on the balcony and stood in the night breeze looking over the city. The lights of the university's pharmacology building blazed brilliantly. Now and then, a car passed below on Konoe Street, but it was a quiet evening with hardly anyone out. Even when I leaned over the railing toward the Kamo River, all I saw were the flickering city lights.

I imagined the four high school students enjoying their fireworks at the temple gate. I could almost smell the gunpowder. Shuuji was probably gazing at the shifting lights, a childlike expression on his face. Naoya would be keeping an eye on the road to make sure the sparklers didn't start a fire. Akizuki would stand there with a scornful smile, like maybe he didn't realize his friends were doing this because they cared about him. Natsuo was hidden behind a veil of smoke.

I imagined her frowning when she noticed me.

○

One day, before heading to Nishida Spirits, I walked over to the Demachi shopping arcade. The covered walkway was packed with people shopping for dinner. I was hungry, so I bought some *takoyaki* before continuing on to the liquor store. The sun was setting, but the heat showed no sign of letting up. Just as I reached the liquor store, Shuuji called from his cell phone to say something had come up and he wanted to delay our lesson a little.

As I slid open the shop's glass door, I was hit with a refreshing gust of cold air from the air conditioner. "This heat, I swear," Shuuji's father said with exasperation, flapping a paper fan as he sat on the wooden ledge in the entryway. His wife was nowhere to be seen. "Shuuji's not back yet. That kid is hopeless."

"No, he called me. I'll eat some *takoyaki* while I wait."

"How can you eat those in this heat?"

I went upstairs. All the windows were shut in Shuuji's room, and the stuffiness and heat had been building all day. I opened a window, but not even the slightest breeze came through.

"Would you like some barley tea?" Naoya asked, coming in with a bottle of cold tea and a glass. In exchange for the tea, I gave him a piping hot *takoyaki*. He sat down cross-legged across from me and stuffed it into his mouth, beads of sweat running down his face. Usually, I viewed him as Shuuji's polar opposite, but as he hunched over, struggling with the hot ball of dough, I could see they were siblings after all.

This was the first time the two of us had talked alone. He always looked people straight in the eye when he spoke to them. It made him seem grown up.

"Is Akizuki still on lockdown?" I asked.

"He's allowed to go out, but he's too stubborn to do it."

"Shuuji told me about what happened before. About the coup d'état and all."

"That's kind of an exaggeration," he said, smiling wryly.

"It sounded rough, though."

"I guess. The older guys said a lot of stuff about us."

"I heard Akizuki went kind of crazy."

"He should have just left them alone. Taking them seriously like that only made things worse. He's like an elementary school kid that way."

The sweat rolling down my back felt like crawling insects and was deeply unpleasant. Now that Naoya's mouth wasn't full of *takoyaki*, his face took on its usual wise appearance. Maybe he was able to remain so calm despite the sweat covering his face because he'd learned to tolerate the heat during practice.

"Shuuji told me you're really good at kendo. He said he was no match for you."

"He's not half bad himself."

"Why are you so good?"

"I don't know. It's kind of reflexive for me. That's all."

"Must feel good."

He tilted his head.

"Have you ever had the feeling that something else is controlling your body, and you're watching from behind?" he asked.

"That's an odd way of putting it. Are you sure you like kendo?"

"I don't know."

I could hear his father stomping around downstairs and shouting. Shuuji had apparently returned.

"I still remember how Shuuji used to cry all the time in elementary school," Naoya said, keeping an ear tuned to the commotion downstairs. "He hated to lose. And he hasn't changed one bit."

"I can see that."

"There are times I envy him for that. It sounds weird, but sometimes I don't like that I practice kendo differently now, that I've stopped doing it the way I did back when I was a kid."

"Doesn't that mean you've matured?"

Naoya smiled bleakly.

"I wouldn't call it that."

I heard someone run heavily up the stairs, shaking the house. As Naoya stood, holding the empty bottle of barley tea, Shuuji opened the door and came in.

"Man, this heat," he moaned, staring at the two of us.

○

That evening, I drank with their father, took a bath at their house, and ended up heading home close to midnight. When I was walking out the door, their father, who had been dozing, jumped up and warned me to be careful.

Walking home, I followed the long wall of the old high school. The street was dim, with only a few streetlamps. The black stains on the wall made me uneasy. As I walked alone through the silence, I thought I saw one of them move. A light breeze rustled the leaves of an inky tree on the far side of the wall, and something ran along one of its branches. In the distance, the light of the vending machines glittered.

I noticed a stick-thin form steadily approaching me. I was certain it was Natsuo, but she walked straight ahead as if she didn't see me. She looked almost like a doll.

"Natsuo," I said. She gave a start and looked at me.

"Teacher."

"It's dangerous to be out by yourself."

"I had an errand to run..."

"Want me to walk you home?"

"No, I'm fine."

She continued walking past me with determination, bound for some mysterious destination.

I bought a can of coffee from the vending machine. When I looked back up, she had vanished from the desolate tunnel of a street. I could hear thunder rumbling softly in the distance. The lightning would probably start soon. I knew I ought to hurry up and get home, but I stood staring down the street, unable to move.

Presently, a long, thin creature came running toward me, as if it was tracing the path Natsuo had walked but in reverse. When it reached a streetlight six or seven paces away, it crouched down, extending only its neck in my direction. Then it grinned silently in the pale fluorescent light.

I threw away my empty can and stepped forward.

○

The rain that had been falling all morning temporarily lifted, leaving a chill in the air.

As I crossed Kojin Bridge and stood waiting for the light to change on Kawaramachi Street, a fine rain misted my face. I had an umbrella with me, but the cool rain felt so good that I didn't put it up. Although I had often wandered around that neighborhood, I'd never gone into Akizuki's temple, so I decided to stop by.

Inside the gate, a stone path led straight ahead toward the main worship hall, with the temple office and priest's family residence sharing a building on the left. There was a walled-in graveyard toward the back of the main hall, to the right. A magnificent camphor tree arched its branches over the temple grounds, as lush as a forest. The rain made a soft hissing sound as it hit the tree's broad leaves. I didn't see anyone else on the grounds.

I circled around the right side of the main hall and spotted Akizuki dangling his legs over the edge of the veranda. When he saw me, he wiggled his eyebrows and called out, "Hey," an ice pop still hanging out of his mouth.

I took off my shoes, pressed my hands on the wooden veranda, and hoisted myself up. The boards were damp with rain, and the smell of old wood wafted from its surface. Akizuki was wearing a T-shirt and shorts, swinging his legs. A thin curl of smoke rose from a mosquito coil burning over a ceramic saucer, and a paperback and a brown sweet bun on a plate lay beside it.

"The temple must be busy with the Bon holiday."

"I was supposed to help, but that's out the window now."

"Because of what happened?"

"Guess so."

"I hear they're still doing the patrols."

"If they're going to do patrols, I wish they'd hurry up and catch the guy."

He rested both hands on the veranda, buried his chin in his chest, and gazed out at the soft rain falling on the temple grounds. His silky hair fell messily over his glasses. I followed his gaze. On the far side of the wall, I could see the rainy skyline and the grove of trees at the Imperial Garden.

"I don't care if people talk about me," Akizuki said. "But I don't like when they blame it on kendo. It's not fair to Takeda-sensei, either. Doing kendo and hitting people with sticks are two totally different things."

"Do you like kendo?" I asked. He nodded. "When I asked Naoya that, he said he wasn't sure."

"He and I are different."

"If you like kendo that much, why did you quit the club?"

He looked at me suspiciously.

"You sure are nosy." He peered at me coolly for a moment, halfway into a bite of his sweet bun, before breaking into a grin. "Anyway, it doesn't matter. I'm sure they told you everything already."

"I heard about the coup d'état."

"Oh, that. I guess we did kick out three seniors we didn't like."

"You kicked them out?"

"I mean, Naoya's pretty harsh. If you're that obvious about it, of course they're gonna hold a grudge."

"But you didn't get along with them, either, right?"

Akizuki tilted his head. "I didn't really care," he muttered. "They did give us a hard time, though. Sometimes I wonder why we put up with it at all. I guess everyone acted like it was normal."

"But you didn't hate them for it?"

"Nah."

"Then why didn't you keep your head down? You could have stayed in the club."

"I wonder." He laughed hollowly, dodging my question. But the eyes staring at me from behind his glasses weren't laughing at all.

"I thought you were taking revenge for Naoya," I said.

"You think someone like me would do that?" He sneered. "You're not a very good judge of character."

"Maybe not."

"Anyway, I kind of don't care anymore. A lot happened last year."

"The older guys beat you up badly, huh?"

Akizuki looked at me and twisted his face into a smile. "Yeah, they did."

"What happened?"

"Let's just leave it at that." He took out a cigarette. "Want one?" he asked, holding it up to me.

"Isn't it a bad idea to smoke here?" I asked, looking around the worship hall.

"It's so damp out, it probably won't burn anyway," Akizuki said, holding it in his mouth to light.

The smoke dissipated into the drizzle.

I didn't know what to say. I sat silently next to him as he smoked. I wanted to leave for Nishida Spirits, but I couldn't stand to just get up and go after our exchange, so I stayed where I was. Feeling strangely stubborn, I gazed out at the rain.

"You smell like an animal," Akizuki mumbled suddenly. I felt a chill run through me. "Natsuo used to smell like that. Back when she still went to the dojo. I liked that smell. I was sad when it left her."

He looked at me, exhaling a mouthful of smoke. His glasses reflected the weak light filtering through the low, leaden clouds. He seemed to be appraising me.

"You're the same."

"The same as what?"

"I can tell. You smell like she did back then."

We stared at each other silently for some time. Eventually, Akizuki's cigarette burned down to the filter, and he tossed it in the saucer holding the mosquito coil.

"You should get going," he said quietly. I nodded. "Naoya and Natsuo will be here soon."

"Are they coming to hang out?"

"They're having a match at the temple."

"Why not at the dojo?"

"Natsuo doesn't want to go back to the dojo. She'll only fight Naoya now."

I stepped off the veranda into my shoes. My backside felt cool and damp from sitting on the wet wood. The rain was falling harder now, so I took my umbrella out of my bag. Akizuki stood up on the veranda and watched me.

"Have you ever seen something like this?" he asked suddenly, moving his hands horizontally to form a long, pipelike shape. "How can I describe it? It's really long and fast, and it hangs around empty lots."

"What could that be, I wonder?"

We stared at each other for a minute until finally he said, "Never mind."

I left the temple.

○

That year, the period between the Gion Festival and the ritual bonfires of the Gozan Okuribi seemed to pass more quickly than ever before. The days felt like they were blurring together in my mind.

When I look back on that summer, images float like tiny islands in the bleak flash of time. Nishida Spirits glowing in the twilight; Shuuji's back, bent over his desk; Naoya stuffing *takoyaki* into his mouth; a group of children swarming around a watermelon out on the street; Akizuki sitting idly on the damp veranda; Natsuo's eyes; a phantom racing through the street at night.

On the evening of the Okuribi, I went out for an aimless stroll. I hadn't particularly planned to watch the bonfires. I figured I'd take a walk and then eat somewhere. Here and there, women in cotton *yukata* could be seen among the crowd. Although the air was still hot and humid, and summer wouldn't end until September, to me, the bonfires always signaled that the season was coming to a close.

I passed Natsuodou. I'd never had a good look at the place, so I peered inside. A light bulb tinted the interior yellow, and while the shop's front was narrow, it stretched back quite a ways. Numerous thin strips of bamboo, apparently used to make kendo swords, were leaning against the wall. I also spotted protective gear and, hanging on the wall, kendo uniforms.

I could see someone moving around in the back of the shop and was about to leave when the person ran up to the glass.

"Hello," Natsuo said, sliding open the door. I nodded at her. She nodded back, her hair swaying.

"Are you out for a walk?" she asked.

"Yeah, going to get some dinner."

"You're not going to watch the bonfires?"

"Who knows, maybe I will."

"You'd better not stay out too late."

I nodded, said good-bye, and walked off. I imagined she must be watching me from behind. I wanted to return her gaze but didn't turn around.

The area around Demachiyanagi Station was crowded, and festival stalls had even been set up outside. I could see the lights of police officers directing traffic. Everyone seemed to be waiting to see the bonfires. After dinner, I walked north along the dark eastern bank of the Takano River. The water looked black. Masses of people were gathered around Mikage Bridge, so I joined the throng and looked up to the east. I could see Mount Daimonji through the gaps between buildings, the flames flickering like red electric lights on its black slope.

Suddenly sensing someone's eyes on me, I glanced to the side. Naoya was standing beyond a clump of people, looking this way. When I raised a hand, he smiled and walked over. I got the vague feeling he'd been watching me.

"Hi," he said.

"Here to see the bonfires?" I asked.

"I came with Natsuo, but we got separated."

We slipped through the crowd and sat down on the riverbank. Normally this would have been a quiet spot, but that evening, it was buzzing with people all the way to the confluence of the Kamo and Takano Rivers. Eventually, I supposed, quiet would return.

"So Akizuki told you Natsuo and I practice kendo at the temple?"

"Yeah."

"Don't tell Shuuji. He gets jealous." After a moment, Naoya said, "Wait a minute," and ran up the riverbank. A few minutes later, he came back with some juice he'd bought at a vending machine. When I offered to pay, he said, "Don't worry about it. My dad gave me the money."

Naoya sat beside me looking at the Takano River.

"The water's so dark," he said.

"Yeah. It's shallow, though."

"A long time ago, I tied up a creature and drowned it in this river."

"Why'd you do something like that?"

"Starting in elementary school, Natsuo had this weird creature she secretly kept as a pet. She likes to wander around by herself, so it must have caught her eye while she was out one day. She secretly started feeding it, and eventually it began prowling around her house. It got really attached to her and wouldn't go away."

"Was it a dog or a cat?"

"Who knows what it was? I sure don't."

Naoya threw a pebble into the dark water.

"Whatever it was, it was creepy. It followed her everywhere—to the dojo, to school, wherever. That went on until she was in her third year of junior high. She's talented, so she handled it well, but we all knew that eventually it would get to be too much. That said, the thing had been with her nonstop since she was a little girl, and it was like her third arm. There was no way she could kill it herself. So Akizuki and I decided to take care of it for her."

The spectators had gone home, and the riverbank was quiet. I held my breath, waiting for Naoya to go on. He took a sip of juice.

"There was a thunderstorm that night. Whenever Natsuo went to sleep, the creature would crawl under the covers with her. That's how we caught it. Then we tied it up, weighted it down, and drowned it in the river from right here on this bank. It was pouring rain, and the river was high, so I was sure it must have died. Afterward, we went back to her house."

"But it didn't die, did it?"

"We told her it was all over and then Akizuki and I left. Later, Akizuki came back here and pulled the thing out of the water."

"Why would he do that?"

"Who knows? He wouldn't say, and I don't understand it. But it was way too much for him to handle. Natsuo was only able to because she's Natsuo."

"I could see that," I said, like I knew what he meant.

"Natsuo tried to kill it herself after that. But she let it go at the last minute. I was injured at the time from my fight at the kendo club, so I couldn't help her. I won't let that happen again."

I saw Natsuo walking toward us down the riverbank. When she spotted us, she grinned and waved.

"That creature is still prowling around the neighborhood," Naoya said, waving back at her. His tone was ominous and cold.

○

Late at night, I got a call from Shuuji.

"Were you sleeping?" he asked. "Are you in your room?"

"Yeah, but I was awake," I answered.

"It got my dad."

"What?"

"The phantom attacker," he said. Then, in a rush, he added, "He's not badly hurt. They just grazed his arm and ran off. Dad said he chased them, but I'm not sure he did. Anyway, they got away."

"I'm glad he's okay."

"Yeah." On the other end of the line, Shuuji was silent for a moment.

"What's wrong?" I asked. He gave a low, canine growl.

"He said the attacker was like a real phantom. Apparently, when he chased them, they glided away like a shadow and vanished. Right away, a big search party went out, but they couldn't find anyone. It's really creepy."

"Hmm."

"Anyway, that's all. You don't need to worry about my dad. Talk to you later."

"Bye."

I hung up.

Now that I wasn't listening to Shuuji's voice, the sound of insects flying around my ear grew deafening.

Moonlight glimmered faintly through cracks between the boards, but as soon as I moved away from them, everything was dark. The smell of decay mixed with the smell of dirt. I reached out a sweaty hand, but my movements didn't feel like my own.

I took a step out of the shadows.

As the darkness of the abandoned house seeped into me, I felt as if my body were a black shadow in the moonlight, stretched long and thin. The empty lot was deserted. I held my breath and took a step forward.

A long-bodied creature was running through the tall, moonlit grass as if leading the way. It stopped and craned its long neck toward me. "Come on," it said.

○

I set out to tutor Shuuji for the last time.

I woke up in the evening and left my apartment on foot beneath a cover of clouds. A tepid breeze was blowing down Konoe Street, and the western sky was tinted reddish purple. The people on the street looked like shadows that had stood up and begun to walk. Looking south from Kojin Bridge, I thought the city lights on either side of the Kamo River seemed fainter than usual. I stopped by the snack shop and bought some of the biscuits Shuuji liked.

The liquor store was closed, so I went in through the house. In the family room, Shuuji's father was watching television and absently rubbing his arm, which was wrapped in bandages. When I said hello, he turned toward me like he was surprised.

"Oh, hello," he said and stared at me intently for a moment.

"Is your arm okay?"

"What?"

Only after I tapped my own arm did he register what I meant. "Oh, it's fine. Look," he said, raising it to show me.

Just then, the front door opened, and Akizuki came in with a loud hello.

"So you're allowed to leave the temple now?" I asked. He looked at me like the question was ridiculous.

"I could've left anytime. I was just being stubborn."

"Then you're done being stubborn?"

"Well, hardly anyone's suspicious of me anymore."

He gestured at the staircase like he wanted me to go up ahead of him.

Upstairs, Akizuki poked his nose into Shuuji's room and sniggered. Then he glanced at me and went into Naoya's room. I could hear Natsuo's voice in there, too. Apparently, they were having a meeting.

I went into Shuuji's room. He was lying spread-eagle on the tatami mats, snoring. I tapped him with my foot, and he sat up, groaning. He looked sweaty and uncomfortable.

Things felt off and unsettled that night, and I suspected neither of us would be able to concentrate. He kept fiddling with his hair, and I didn't feel much like reading.

"Let's take a break," I said. He let out a loud, warm breath and slumped against the wall next to me. "Have some of these," I said, holding out some health biscuits. He grinned and placed a few on his palm.

"So Naoya and the others are hanging out tonight?" I asked, taking a draw on my cigarette.

"Wonder why they're being so sneaky." Shuuji angled an ear toward Naoya's room, but we couldn't hear anything. "I don't like it," he said. "Why're they leaving me out?"

"Oh, stop sulking."

"They did it the other night on patrol, too. It's always been like that. I mean, when Natsuo quit kendo, I was the only one who didn't know about it."

He looked up at the ceiling. I could see him rolling the biscuit around in his mouth.

"Back then, Natsuo came over and cried in Naoya's room. I thought they were fighting, but maybe she was just unsure what to do."

"She was crying?"

"Yeah. I eavesdropped a little."

"You shouldn't do that."

"Don't tell Naoya." After a moment, he shook his head. "It's a real waste. She was so good at kendo. She didn't need to quit."

"Have some more. As many as you want," I said, placing some more biscuits in his large palm. He funneled them into his mouth, chuckling.

○

It was past ten, so I decided to wrap up our session. Shuuji's father didn't invite me to drink with him that night, and the time had passed quietly. Even though Naoya, Akizuki, and Natsuo were supposedly in Naoya's room, we couldn't hear them talking. I strained my ears now and then while I was tutoring Shuuji, but I didn't hear a thing.

When I went out into the hallway, Shuuji followed me. He looked into Naoya's room and asked, "Where are Naoya and Akizuki?" Natsuo, who was the only one left, seemed to say something in response. I glanced back as I started down the stairs. Shuuji followed me, shrugging.

"I guess Naoya and Akizuki went out," he said.

"I didn't even notice them leave."

"I don't get it. I bet they're up to something they're not supposed to again."

"So Natsuo's up there by herself?"

"Yeah."

I glanced over his shoulder down the hallway. Naoya's door was open slightly, and Natsuo was watching us through the crack.

When we got downstairs, Shuuji's father wasn't in the family room anymore.

"Wonder where he went with his arm still messed up," Shuuji muttered.

Shuuji seemed like he wanted to say something as he saw me off at the entryway. He put his shoes on and followed me outside.

"See you later," I said, planning to leave, but he stopped me. "Listen," he said, then paused. The warm breeze tousled his unruly hair, giving him a helpless, anxious look. I stopped mid-step and turned back to him.

"What's wrong?" I asked

"Go straight home and don't stop anywhere, okay?" he said.

I walked away through the tepid, ominous air. A sweet smell like fruit hung over the street.

○

The thick gray clouds covering the sky were uncannily bright, perhaps lit up by the glow of the city. The sweet smell was getting stronger. I figured the rain would come soon.

I slipped through the quiet night streets. Eventually, I turned down that same narrow alley and emerged in the backyard of the abandoned house.

The city lights shone faintly over the walls surrounding the yard. The grass rustled with each step I took. Its scent, mixed with that of the rain, hung in the dusky light. Bugs flew relentlessly around my face. When I squinted into the shadows, I could make out the dry, overgrown well.

I heard the sound of my own breath mixed with the buzzing of the insects. But when I listened more closely, I began to get the sense that I wasn't the one making the sound. The sweat dripping from my temples felt like insects crawling down my face.

When I glanced at the corrugated plastic covering the old well, I found the long-bodied creature curled on top of it. It lifted its face toward me, its white teeth gleaming in the darkness. It made a *shi-shi-shi* sound when it breathed, like it was laughing.

I walked up to the well and put my hand on the lid. Gently, I removed it, and a deeper darkness opened up below. I reeled in the plastic rope hanging from the rim and grabbed the wooden sword from out of the well.

The creature had been twisting around beside me in the grass, but now it stopped and gazed up at the abandoned house. Although the house should have been empty, a small light was moving inside. Gripping the wooden sword, I hid in the shadow of a bush. The light swayed two or three times, then went out. No one appeared.

The bright, reddish sky made me uneasy. Somewhere in the distance, thunder was rumbling.

Time passed.

I heard someone's footsteps part the grass near the house and pass the bush where I was hiding. They were smoking. I stuck my head out from the bush and saw the thin form of a teenage boy with his back to me. I watched him pass down the alley toward the street before I slid out from the shadows.

As always, the creature walked ahead of me.

○

I could see the boy walking down the dim street.

He seemed to be heading for the high school. Just before turning the corner, he threw his cigarette into the street. The butt rolled across the dark asphalt, throwing off tiny sparks. I stomped it out before following him around the corner.

His path traced the long wall of the high school. I watched him, hiding in the shadows of the wall. He stopped, and an orange light glowed at his fingertips. He was about to light another cigarette.

Making my way along the wall, I approached him.

The instant before I brought down my sword, someone cried in a stifled voice, "Akizuki!" The light at his fingertips suddenly went out, and he leaped forward. My sword sliced the air.

As I stumbled forward, propelled by momentum, I heard footsteps running toward me from behind. I spun around and jumped to the opposite side of the alley. I heard a wooden sword cut through the air behind me. I glanced over my shoulder and swept my sword back, knocking away a thrust from out of the darkness. I leaped to the side to gain some distance and thrust again. My opponent, who had been about to fly at me again, held back.

In the darkness, I saw Naoya's face. He was standing still, his wooden sword raised. Akizuki was behind him, looking at me.

"Teacher, please get ahold of yourself," Naoya said quietly. "Do you recognize us?"

Instead of answering, I let out a bestial growl. No words came from my mouth.

"It's no good, Naoya. He can't understand what we're saying," Akizuki said. "He's just like I was."

I gripped the sword in my right hand and thrust it toward Naoya, dropping my stance.

It glanced off Naoya's sword and almost struck him, but he dodged. "Over here!" he bellowed, and Akizuki circled around behind me. I moved to swing at Naoya again, but before I could, his sword struck my solar plexus. I fell to my knees. Nausea overwhelmed me, and tears seeped from my eyes. I couldn't see.

I grasped Naoya's sword with one hand.

Then I thrust my own sword over my shoulder at random and felt it hit home. I heard Akizuki's muffled scream behind me. Naoya glanced at him, and in that instant, I knocked his sword out of his hands. Then I struck him on the temple.

He closed his eyes and toppled over sideways. After that, he stayed on the ground, unmoving.

I took a breath, straightened my back, and looked behind me.

Akizuki was curled on the ground with his hand pressed to his mouth, his fingers wet with blood. I took his sword and threw it over the wall of the old high school. I looked down at him, aimed for the back of the hand he'd used to hold his sword, and swung. When I brought my sword back up, he began to cry.

Suddenly, the staticky noise that had been swirling around me stopped, and everything went silent. The only sounds were my own beast-like breaths and Akizuki's groans.

The street flashed as bright as midday, like a light had been switched on. There was a deafening noise like a huge tree cleaving in half. Large raindrops began to fall, as if the bottom had fallen out of the sky, and mist rose on the sidewalk. The two boys on the ground looked as if they were wrapped in cotton.

Rain dripped from my chin like tears.

The lightning made my heart race.

I stood stock-still as the thunder rumbled, looking across the alley.

Natsuo was standing in the middle of the street.

The rain beat down on us so hard that it hurt, blurring the asphalt with spray. Blue lightning illuminated her drenched form, the wooden sword in her right hand glistening. Her thin shirt was pasted to her body, making its curves stand out like fruit. Her body seemed to writhe as it breathed in the scent of the rain that saturated everything around us.

I took a deep breath, grasped my wet sword, and started running toward her. The sound of rain engulfed the street. It smelled sweet.

When I struck her, her body flew into the air.

Out of the corner of my eye, I saw the creature, wet with rain, turn around.

The Water God

I haven't been to many wakes or funerals.

"At my age, it's nothing but funerals," my father muttered as he slipped his arms through the sleeves of his mourning jacket, but I can't yet imagine what that's like. Even if I do go to a funeral, I just do what I'm told, pass the time with my head bowed meekly, and then quietly go home.

The story I'm about to tell took place on the day of my grandfather's wake five years ago.

When I recall that night in late summer, the image of a long, aging tunnel always rises in my mind's eye. The curving walls are made of brick, and when I touch them, they are cold as ice. Four men are passing fearfully through this tunnel. Because it is pitch-black inside, we have to feel our way forward, which sometimes makes us mistake the long, straight tube for a maze. Other times, we stand rooted in place, convinced that someone, or something, is lurking deep in the darkness.

And always, inside the tunnel, is the sound of overflowing water.

○

My grandfather lived alone in a mansion in the Shishigatani neighborhood along Kyoto's eastern hills.

At one point, there was talk of my uncle Kouichirou's family moving in with him, but my grandfather rejected the idea. He refused to give in even after he had a stroke and could no longer get around very well. Only after my uncle bowed his head and begged him, and Dr. Yano, the family physician, repeatedly and patiently persuaded him, did he agree to let Uncle Kouichirou's daughter Misato pay daily visits to care for him.

Oddly enough, my grandfather nevertheless wanted me to attend a university in Kyoto and live in the city. He offered me a room in his mansion and even said he'd pay my school fees, but I didn't take him up on it. Not only would it have been suffocating to spend my university days living with my grandfather, but I was also hesitant to impose on my uncle's family. Against my grandfather's wishes, I enrolled in a university in Osaka.

In spring, after the entrance ceremony was over, I went to visit him. It was the first time I'd crossed his threshold alone. I remember being so nervous, I could feel my spine stiffen.

Compared to the chilly Japanese-style room where he received me, the garden was blindingly bright. The cherry blossoms were falling in flurries, and a spring breeze blew them in from the veranda. My grandfather brought out some sake to celebrate my matriculation, and we drank it as we watched the weeping cherry tree scatter torrents of petals. Afterward, he sat with arms crossed and listened as I discussed beginning university.

Even after I finished, he remained silent. I got the feeling that his grandson refusing his choice of school was not the sole reason his face was so grim as he wordlessly stared at the old pond in the garden. I think, perhaps, he was listening to the uncanny sound of water echoing from the depths of his belly.

○

When he got the news that my grandfather was in critical condition, my father left for Kyoto right away. My mother followed him the next day. When I got home from school, the house was silent. A brief note from my mother was lying on the living room table. In my room, the suit I'd worn to my high school graduation was laid out along with a change of clothes for staying overnight.

I took the Keihan Electric Railway from Hirakata toward Kyoto.

As we passed the foothills of Mount Otoko and crossed the Kizu River, the sky seemed to abruptly darken. The rumble of the train grew louder as it crossed the river. By the time we had passed the Tanba Bridge, all I could see were city lights streaming through the twilight. My vacant face floated in the dark glass across the aisle. I remembered that when I was a boy, my grandfather had scolded me for just such a vacant expression. "Stop making that idiotic face," he'd said. Even now, if I don't watch myself, I still slip into it. My grandfather's reprimand had no effect.

I got off at the Keihan Sanjo station and went up to street level. On the other side of the Kamo River, the brilliant lights of the entertainment district glittered like a dream. It was the weekend, so more people seemed to be out and about. I boarded a bus headed east. Pressing my cheek against the window, I gazed up at the sky. A lopsided moon was floating in the inky eastern sky.

○

I got off the bus at Jodoji and made my way into the quiet neighborhood. My grandfather's mansion was a short walk east. As I passed the rows of houses, I could hear a muffled murmur. Beneath the mansion's stone wall, the Lake Biwa Canal passed through on its way from Nanzenji. Bright light seeped from the far side of the wooden fence, and the leaves of the old cherry tree were visible above it. The line of people in dark clothes, come to give their condolences, stretched all the way to the little bridge spanning the canal.

When I finally managed to break through the wall of people and pass under the heavy, covered gate, I saw that a small reception table had been set up. The familiar man behind it was bowing his head to the visitors. It was Uncle Koujirou, sporting a mustache he hadn't had when I last saw him, during the New Year holiday. As I was hesitating about what to do, he spotted me over his glasses and pressed his lips together in a smile. I gave him a small bow, then continued onto the property.

A lamp had been placed in the corner of the big garden with its old cherry tree, and it cast a shadow play of the mourning procession. I figured they must be neighbors or people my grandfather had known from work, but I couldn't tell who was who. Some smiled quietly, and others remained reserved as they exchanged words in strange voices, neither loud nor quiet. A few pointed at the surface of the pond as if searching for something. Others peered around in admiration at the trees in the garden or drank tea by a table set up on the lawn.

The screens were open into one of the rooms facing the garden, where it seemed my grandfather's altar had been set up. As I glanced around, trying to figure out what to do, my mother passed me carrying a teapot. When I called out to her, she leaned in and whispered that there was seating for relatives in the room facing the garden, and my father was in there.

I took off my shoes in the entryway and went inside.

Misato poked her head out of the dining room and bowed her head toward me. She was the cousin who had been taking care of my grandfather. She was a round, cheerful person like her father, Uncle Kouichirou, but tonight even she looked solemn.

When I stepped into the room, where a tarp had been laid over the tatami mats, I saw my father and Uncle Kouichirou sitting on folding chairs near the altar, talking. My father saw me and gestured for me to join them. I could feel the stares of the other family members seated in front of the shrine shift in my direction. Other than my uncles' families, our only relatives were a few people living in Osaka, and the makeup of the group seemed about the same as the one that had gathered for the New Year.

"Hey!" Uncle Kouichirou said. His face already looked flushed from drinking, and he was smiling like we'd just bumped into each other on the street.

"Hello," I said, bowing my head.

"I thought I wouldn't see you again until next New Year."

"I know."

"You're staying over tonight, right?"

"Yes."

"Then let's have a good long talk later."

Just then, an elderly neighbor named Mr. Hisatani came over and whispered, "Kouichirou, the priest is here."

"I'll be right there," my uncle replied and left the room with the older man.

I sat down in the folding chair next to my father and asked, "Are you staying up all night?"

"No," he said, shaking his head slightly as he stared at the altar. "But there's a lot to discuss. It could go a bit late."

In contrast to Uncle Kouichirou, my father looked haggard as he sat in the folding chair, gazing at the altar. His arms, which were draped listlessly on his knees, appeared much weaker than usual, and huddled there, he seemed almost like a fragile young man of my own age.

I stared at the altar. In the portrait, my grandfather's brows were deeply furrowed as he glared forcefully into empty space. I suspected my father and his brothers had selected this terrifying photograph intentionally, striking a cold fear in the hearts of everyone gathered.

○

While the sutras were being recited, the mourners in their black clothes came up one at a time to light incense. After that, my father, uncles, mother, and other close relatives still seemed busy with various tasks, so I slipped out of the altar room.

At the end of a long corridor extending from the entryway was the door to the dining room. To its right was a staircase to the second floor. After that, the corridor turned left and wrapped all the way around the courtyard. Enclosed by the sliding glass doors of the corridor on all four sides, this courtyard was about the size of eight tatami mats, its mossy ground illuminated by the light spilling through the glass. I could see the small shrine where my grandfather never failed to offer his prayers.

As I walked down the corridor on the south side of the courtyard, I realized my grandfather's altar must be on the other side of the screen to my side, giving me the odd sense that I was backstage at the funeral. I kept walking until I got back to where I'd started, by the stairs. The lights were on in all the rooms surrounding the courtyard, just like at New Year's, except that they were silent.

I climbed the dark stairs to the second floor. My plan was to hide out up there until things quieted down below. The upstairs was dark and hot and permeated by the smell of the aging house. At the end of the wood-plank corridor, I could see the door to my grandfather's study.

I stepped into the Western-style room and flipped the switch on the wall. An orangish glow filled the space, making the surface of the oval table in the center glisten darkly as if it were wet. The floor, which measured around eight tatami mats, was covered with red cloth. As a child, I had seen my father and uncles talking to my grandfather in this room. I remembered how the bluish smoke they exhaled would hover around the old-fashioned lampshade. This was also where my uncles would gather for secretive conversations.

Once, when no one was there, I snuck in and stroked the red fabric floor covering. The shutters were closed, and although it was afternoon, the study was dim. I was terrified. I don't remember why I did it. I may have been sulking because my father or mother had gotten mad at me. The cloth-covered floor seemed damp, and I felt my palm getting wet, but I sat there stroking it for a long time. Only when I heard someone climbing the stairs did I snap out of my reverie, and I must have fled the room. I don't remember who was on the stairs. All I remember clearly is the sensation of the cloth-covered floor beneath my palm.

I sat down in the old chair and smoked a cigarette, just like my father and uncle had done in the past. I tried exhaling a mouthful of wispy smoke in the direction of the lamp. In the center of the table was a cloudy indigo glass bottle. Strangely, although not a drop of water remained, the cut flowers inside were extraordinarily beautiful.

I killed time smoking a few cigarettes as the first floor gradually grew quiet.

○

I heard someone climbing the stairs. The door to the study was open a crack. As I watched the door, smoking another cigarette, Uncle Koujirou quietly pushed it open and walked in. He stared at me from behind his glasses like the light was too bright.

"So this is where you were," he said, smiling, and sat down across from me at the table. "You're still underage, aren't you? You shouldn't be smoking."

I smiled. My uncle took out a cigarette and puffed on it, though he didn't seem to find the taste very appealing. My smoke and his smoke rose together and wound around the lamp.

"They don't need you downstairs?" I asked.

"Come on—don't I get to rest a little?" he asked, looking around the room. "I heard that in the old days, scholars and artists used to gather here and dine. That was before we were born. Kazuko used to talk about it sometimes."

Kazuko was the woman who had overseen housekeeping at the mansion when my father and his brothers were kids. She'd lost her husband in the war and, after that, lived for many years in the mansion. My father had talked about her a number of times.

"What are we going to do tonight?" I asked.

"There'll be a lot to do tomorrow, so everyone else should sleep. Kouichirou, Shigeo, and I will take shifts staying up."

"That sounds like a lot of trouble."

"Oh, the sake will get us through. And we have interesting plans for tonight."

"What plans?"

"You didn't hear about it from Shigeo?" my uncle asked, puffing out some smoke. "Later tonight, someone from Hourendou is supposed to come over."

"Hou-ren-dou?"

"It was a favorite shop of Dad's for years. They're bringing over something he left in their care."

"What is it?"

"No one knows. According to Kouichirou, it's a family heirloom."

Several times when I was in elementary school, my grandfather had taken me into his storehouse. All I remember is that the cool, dim building was nearly empty inside, with a number of identical boxes lined up. I don't think I had much interest at the time. I had a feeling my grandfather had shown me something in the storehouse, but I couldn't remember what it was.

"You should put in an appearance. Dad would be pleased."

I felt some interest in this family heirloom that Hourendou, or whoever they were, was bringing over.

○

After the ceremonies for the wake ended, the mourners headed home.

While my mother and some other relatives were in the kitchen making the evening meal, we cleaned up around the altar and rolled up the tarp.

"Since you'll be using this again tomorrow, why don't you just leave it where it is?" Mr. Hisatani asked.

"We're having some drinks in here tonight," Uncle Kouichirou said. "Call it a memorial service."

"I'll bet the old man will be jealous."

"Well, Dad can't exactly complain anymore."

"I wouldn't be surprised if he stuck his head out and gave you a piece of his mind."

The man from the funeral home came over and started discussing the next day's plans with Uncle Kouichirou and my father. Uncle Koujirou brought out a little desk, set the offering container on it, and began writing something down in a notebook.

I stood on the veranda, which had been left open, and stared out at the pond in the garden. The fluorescent light from the veranda lit up the rocks around the pond and made the surface of the water glisten white. Behind me, I heard Uncle Koujirou ask in a shrill voice, "Wasn't there a safe in this house?"

"I think there's one in the study," Uncle Kouichirou answered. I heard Uncle Koujirou leave the room. My father and the others were still standing around talking.

After the meeting about the next day was over, we had a light meal in another room.

Calm voices mixed with the sound of clinking dishes for a cordial family dinner. Even after nine, it still felt hot and humid, and everyone took off their jackets. There was no sign of autumn despite the fact that it was almost the middle of September.

After dinner, Mr. Hisatani stood up and said he was heading home for the night. My father and his brothers all stood up as well and bowed their heads in unison. I watched their identical gestures from the edge of the group.

"There'll be plenty to do tomorrow, so don't wear yourselves out tonight," the elderly man said quietly.

My father saw him off at the gate. When he returned, he asked Uncle Kouichirou, "Mr. Hisatani doesn't know about tonight?"

"No, we're the only ones who know," my uncle answered.

I guessed they were referring to the arrangements with Hourendou.

○

Each family group retired to the room they were usually given. After seeing that everyone else was in bed, my father and uncles settled in to keep the incense burning, a bottle of sake beside them. As Uncle Koujirou came out of the dining room dangling the large bottle, my aunt had intercepted him and warned him not to do anything that would interfere with the next day's events.

I took my leave for a moment and headed to our room on the west side of the courtyard. As I finished changing, my father slid open the screen, his jacket and tie in hand, and told me to come join the brothers. We walked down the corridor surrounding the courtyard and crossed paths with my mother, who apparently was on her way back from taking a shower. "Don't overdo it," she told us.

"We'll take turns sleeping," my father answered.

In the dining hall, my uncles were piling the remnants of the evening meal onto trays. They each carried one back to the altar room.

Uncle Kouichirou went up to the altar with the sake in his hands and sat down with his knees tucked below him and his back ramrod straight, like he was attending a ceremony.

"I will do the honors," he said, tone careful and courteous, setting the bottle in front of the altar. It must have been my grandfather's everyday brand. He didn't like switching up the flavor he was used to, and he wouldn't accept any substitutes.

When my father and his brothers finally started drinking, they seemed self-conscious in front of the altar and didn't say much at first. They were probably also tired from the past two days. Even the ever-lively Uncle Kouichirou was acting subdued.

"We don't have to be so mopey, do we?" Uncle Koujirou said.

"That wasn't my intention," Uncle Kouichirou said.

"You're the one who suggested we drink in front of Dad, Koujirou," my father said, smiling wryly. "So you're responsible for cheering us all up."

"I remember when Dad was alive," Uncle Koujirou said, looking up at the altar with a frown. Behind his glasses, the area around his eyes was already slightly flushed. "He used to rib the hell out of me about sake."

"You mean about drinking at dinner?" Uncle Kouichirou asked, laughing. "You always used to have half a cup."

"He used to say I might as well not drink at all."

"He was right," my father said.

"Dad always seemed to enjoy his sake. He downed it like water," Uncle Kouichirou said. "I wonder if it even tasted good when he drank it that fast."

Uncle Koujirou was shoving leftover simmered vegetables into his mouth and chewing them enthusiastically. After noisily gulping down his food, he glanced at the dark veranda, sniffing the smoke from the mosquito coil as it drifted quietly toward him.

Uncle Kouichirou clapped loudly, taking out a feeble mosquito as it flew past.

"The mosquitos are getting weak," he mumbled.

"It's still so hot, though," my father replied.

"I guess the heat wore these guys out, too," Uncle Kouichirou said pityingly, scraping the corpse of the mosquito off his palm.

○

My grandfather was a hard drinker. He was the kind of mythical man who drank without pausing to breathe, consuming alcohol so fast, no one could possibly keep up. But even though he drank with bottomless capacity, none of his sons could ever remember seeing him drunk.

By the time I was old enough to be aware of it, the waterfall of alcohol he once consumed had thinned considerably. Still, every evening as dusk fell, he would sit looking out at the garden, drinking glass after glass alone in silence. His bony, emaciated back was always pulled up perfectly straight, as if he was following some code of etiquette. He never looked very drunk when he finished for the evening, either.

His hard-drinking blood must have ended with him, however, because it never reached us. But my father and his brothers remembered his copious alcohol consumption with nostalgia, and though their tolerance was poor, they all liked to drink. Once drunk, though, they couldn't maintain their composure as he had, and they often embarrassed themselves.

Uncle Koujirou was the worst. Maybe it was inevitable, because his job required drinking with university students. Before his retirement, rumors of his extraordinary and disgraceful behavior were often a topic of conversation and a cause for wry laughter.

Uncle Kouichirou and my father couldn't hold their drink,

either, but they didn't let themselves go as often as their middle brother. They were happy, pleasant drunks.

It was Uncle Koujirou who had suggested they all drink together in front of the altar while they waited for the person from Hourendou to arrive, and his two brothers had agreed. Needless to say, nobody actually thought my grandfather would stick his head out of his coffin and complain.

○

Gradually, the little party started to gather momentum, and everyone looked happier. The conversation was bouncing along. It was amusing to watch the three men's faces grow increasingly red.

Uncle Kouichirou told us about the time my father got into an argument with my grandfather and left the house. He freeloaded off Uncle Kouichirou for a while and didn't reconcile with my grandfather until after I was born. My uncle wove in the story of how my parents met, and he made it sound so romantic and old-fashioned that I felt embarrassed. Maybe because he was drunk, my father didn't try to contradict him. I wasn't sure how much of it he was making up.

"Dad sold off Grandad's collection to pay for your school fees and everything else," Uncle Kouichirou said. "I had my eye on that stuff, but before I knew it, the storehouse was empty."

"Most of it was junk. It must have been hard to sell," my father said, smiling.

"It was. That storehouse was full of stuff like magic lanterns and creepy taxidermy... Dubious items like that don't bring in much money."

"I remember that taxidermy!" Uncle Koujirou said, slapping his knee. "What the hell was that anyway? It was so weird."

"Do you remember it, Shigeo? It was some kind of creepy animal with a long body..."

"How could I forget?"

"When we did something bad, Dad used to shut us up in the back room with that thing."

"I still have nightmares about it. I'm all alone staring at it, and ever so slowly, it turns its taxidermy neck, looks at me, and grins."

"It was really frightening."

"I think Hourendou took that one. I was so relieved."

"The collection was completely incoherent, but there were some good things in there," Uncle Koujirou said. "Like that set of dragon netsuke—that was incredible, wasn't it?"

"Dad pushed Hourendou into buying a mountain of junk off him, but I'll bet they made their money back and then some."

"The thing they're bringing over tonight, was that something they bought back then?" I asked.

"No, this is different. Apparently, it's something Dad entrusted to them specially," Uncle Kouichirou answered.

"Wonder what it is," Uncle Koujirou said, pouring more sake.

It was then that the wall clock threw a bucket of cold water over the lively conversation.

The four of us fell silent and listened to the old-fashioned sound of the chime. The clock's black hour hand pointed to eleven. My mother and cousins must have all been asleep in their rooms by then. The mansion was hushed, and I imagined the sporadic rings of the clock rolling down the long, dark corridor. Listening silently to that sound, I felt in my bones that I was at a wake.

"I wonder if everything's okay," Uncle Kouichirou said, like he'd been waiting for the chime to finish ringing. "They said they were coming at eleven."

○

Dr. Yano, the family doctor, was a friend of my grandfather's from their high school days before the war. By the time my grandfather died, Dr. Yano's son and grandchildren had taken over his clinic, and he had taken a step back. But as my grandfather's friend and family doctor, he attended his bedside in the mansion until the end.

Dr. Yano had always combined casual conversation with house calls to his friend, but my grandfather rarely let himself be examined. "Talking with you is enough," he would say, trying to dodge his checkups. But Dr. Yano was intimately familiar with the stubborn streak that had passed like an iron rod through my grandfather's life ever since his high school days. He would smile and pretend to accept my grandfather's willfulness, but now and then the two would butt heads, Dr. Yano using his responsibility as a doctor as his shield. As a result, the pair had argued a number of times. After going in circles for a while, my grandfather's taut cheeks would relax into a smile, and he would slip Dr. Yano's first name into the conversation as a signal that he was letting down his guard. If my grandfather had any friends he felt able to lean on, it was Dr. Yano and Mr. Hisatani.

Dr. Yano heard about the "family heirloom" from my grandfather shortly after the end of the war. My grandfather told him it had been in the mansion ever since the family's progenitor, Naojirou Higuchi, dug it up. When Dr. Yano asked what it was, my grandfather only smiled suggestively. All he would say was that he'd found where his father had hidden it.

Mr. Hisatani heard the same story. He tried to needle more details out of my grandfather, but he wouldn't say anything definite. He only insisted with peculiar force that he did not intend to give it to his sons. He didn't think they could handle it. Mr. Hisatani tried to convince him he was wrong, but my grandfather refused to change his mind. He insisted it was too much for them.

The business associates who visited the mansion often talked about this family heirloom my grandfather was hiding. Some of them asked him about it point-blank over meals in the second-floor study, but he would grin and refuse to answer, which only made them more interested.

Others made overblown speculations about it being some sort of treasure his ancestors had dug up. Perhaps the riches of some court noble, buried long ago and then forgotten, had been rediscovered when the mansion was built. Or was it the war chest of a patriot in the Meiji Restoration or maybe the buried gold of Toyotomi Hideyoshi? My grandfather seemed to enjoy listening to these outlandish theories.

Several antique dealers heard the rumors and came poking around, but he turned them all away.

However, after my grandfather's second wife, Hanae, died, he changed completely and stopped talking about the mysterious heirloom. Whenever someone jokingly mentioned it, he would shut them up with a cold glare. Soon enough, joking about the family heirloom became taboo.

○

"So you don't know anything about the family heirloom?" my father asked.

"When I was young, I had all kinds of fantasies about it," Uncle Kouichirou said bashfully. "Like the others, I was convinced Naojirou had dug something up."

"Back in the Meiji era, you mean?"

"What Kouichirou thought was that he found a treasure and pocketed it on the sly," Uncle Koujirou teased. "Romantic tale, right?"

"I don't know much about Naojirou, but he sounds like a difficult guy. It wouldn't be a stretch to imagine him doing something like that," Uncle Kouichirou said, crossing his arms.

From time to time when they were young, my uncles would think about the hidden heirloom. They attempted to wheedle fragments of information out of Mr. Hisatani and Dr. Yano that might serve as clues. When they were in university, the two of them plotted to sneak into the storehouse when their father was away. But of course, whatever it was wasn't going to be labeled, and they weren't able to figure out what among the disorganized piles of stuff it might be.

Over time, as money grew tight, antiques began to flow out of the mansion like water from a tilted cup. The episode my uncle had recounted about selling off their grandfather's collection took place around that time, too. Once the masses of old junk were gone, nothing left looked particularly like an heirloom—the item my grandfather called our family's guardian deity. It's quite possible that he casually sold it off in the course of cleaning out the storehouse. Or maybe the story he told in the past was only his version of a joke, concocted merely because he enjoyed hearing his friends make off-target guesses and watch greedy antique dealers come knocking.

At some point, my uncles lost interest in the family treasure.

"Just when I'd completely forgotten about it, we got that call," Uncle Kouichirou said.

As my father and his brothers were making arrangements for the funeral with Mr. Hisatani, the phone in the mansion rang. Uncle Kouichirou answered. "I'm calling from Hourendou," the young woman on the end of the line said. He remembered the name. It was that of the little curio shop that had been in charge of clearing out the mountains of stuff in the storehouse.

"I received a call from your house this morning, but I won't be able to come until quite late…," the woman said.

My uncle was flustered.

"Would it be all right if I come over around eleven tonight?" she continued.

"Excuse me but…on what business?"

"I was told this morning to return the item that your father had entrusted to us."

"Ah!" he exclaimed. The *family heirloom* that Uncle Kouichirou had completely forgotten resurfaced in his memory.

"Hourendou sure has a surprisingly good recollection of something that happened a generation ago," my father said. Uncle Kouichirou tilted his head.

"She said someone called that morning, but I don't remember making a call like that. I thought maybe Dad had asked Misato to do it, but she said she'd never heard of Hourendou."

"Then who contacted them?" my father asked.

"I don't know."

“I only heard about it when Kouichirou called me,” my father said.

“And I’d forgotten all about it until he told me,” Uncle Koujirou said.

“It’s strange.”

The brothers tilted their heads and puffed on their cigarettes. I didn’t have anything to do, so I poured myself some sake and sipped at it.

“Big drinker, eh?” Uncle Koujirou said, squinting at me like the light was too bright.

○

The originator of the Kyoto branch of the Higuchi family was Naojirou Higuchi. He moved there from Tokyo, where he had studied mechanical engineering. After finishing school, he worked as an engineer on the excavation of the Lake Biwa Canal between Kyoto and Shiga Prefectures. He was my great-great-grandfather.

After the Meiji Restoration, the emperor moved his residence to Tokyo while Kyoto remained mired in the chaos of the recent political upheaval. A number of initiatives were undertaken to increase its appeal as a city of modern engineering. The Lake Biwa Canal was likely the largest of these plans. Later, a second canal was built, but the first one alone took a full five years to complete, from 1885 through 1890.

During construction, in order to minimize the time needed to dig the tunnel, vertical shafts were dug in advance along the planned route. Whenever the diggers hit a water vein, huge quantities of water would gush into the shaft. There was far too much to remove by hand, so a steam pump had to be used. Naojirou had apparently helped maintain these pumps. Among the many anecdotes surrounding the construction of the Lake Biwa Canal, those about the battle against the natural springs are especially famous. In one case, an utterly exhausted manager even committed suicide by throwing himself into one of the shafts after installing a pump.

No one knows exactly what Naojirou did down there by lamplight as water gushed out of the ground. Neither my great-grandfather nor my grandfather said much about their predecessors, and all the stories about Naojirou are terribly vague. Perhaps there was something in his background that they didn't want to talk about.

○

Sitting beside my uncles, I imagined that dark, cold shaft. Somewhere in the distance, I could hear water running, probably a neighbor using their shower or bath. But it wasn't so far off, and gradually it blended with the images of those sopping wet Meiji-era men building the Lake Biwa Canal, giving me the odd sense I was there with them. Despite the late hour, hot, humid air clung heavily to my neck, and yet a chill ran down my spine at the vision of the deep black shaft and the water that filled it.

"Naojirou's treasure, eh?" Uncle Koujirou muttered, rubbing his red face with both hands.

"I figured that must be what Hourendou is bringing over," Uncle Kouichirou said, then fixed his gaze on me. "Did Dad tell you anything about it?"

"No, nothing comes to mind," I said.

"Nothing at all?"

"You went to see Dad by yourself that one time. He didn't mention it then?" my father asked.

"No, he never mentioned Hourendou."

"I guess we'll have to wait until that woman shows up to find out," Uncle Koujirou said.

Uncle Kouichirou took a cigarette out of his breast pocket and lit it.

"We might as well play one hundred stories or something, then."

"You mean where we blow out a candle after each story?"

"That's not a bad idea. Anyone have one? One about Dad would be good, given the situation."

"What if I tell the story of the first time I got drunk?" Uncle Koujirou said. "I was with Dad that time."

"Oh, I know that story," Uncle Kouichirou said.

Uncle Koujirou poured more sake, as if he was cherishing each drop.

○

When Koujirou was in high school, his nickname was Fish Paste. His classmates gave him the name because he was always sitting at his desk, studying his textbooks through glasses like thick, round slices of fish paste. Kouichirou, who went to the same school, heard it and promptly told everyone at home.

This spurred Koujirou on to crazy new levels of bookishness, and he began to go around with a tormented look on his face. Their father didn't take much notice of his sons, but at the time, Kazuko was still living at the mansion, and she became quite worried. She was like a second mother to my uncles, who had lost their real mother when they were very young. But no matter what she said,

Koujirou wouldn't give up his obsessive study habits. Finally, she went to their father. He ignored her. As for Kouichirou, he didn't hesitate to shout, "Fish Paste!" at Koujirou's back whenever he left the table early to continue studying. Kazuko was the only one concerned.

In the summer of his second year of high school, Koujirou collapsed from exhaustion. It seemed the taut wire of his nerves had finally snapped. Unable to get out of bed, he lay staring at the wood grain on the ceiling. When he finally managed to get up, he sat leaning against a post, staring at the garden.

One bright, sunny afternoon when the cicadas were calling incessantly, my grandfather took the dazed Koujirou on an outing.

He didn't say where they were going. Koujirou stumbled shakily after his father, who was strolling along in a casual kimono, his glossy black walking stick shining in the afternoon sun. They walked slowly along the canal and then entered the grounds of Nanzenji Temple, backgrounded by dense forest. The calls of the cicadas were becoming more insistent. The redbrick aqueduct arched quietly behind the trees. *Up there, water from Lake Biwa must be gushing along*, Koujirou thought to himself. *I wonder what it would be like to climb up and throw myself into that cool water.*

His father entered a large, elegant old Japanese restaurant next to Nanzenji that itself resembled a temple. Koujirou had never been anywhere like that, and he followed along, craning his neck around as he went.

They were led to a large tatami-lined room on the second floor. The windows were wide open, and past the railing, the deep-green leaves of the trees that cocooned the restaurant glittered in the sun. A cool breeze drifted across the room and down the corridor.

Koujirou drank alcohol for the first time in that room. His father tipped back his cup so casually, but when Koujirou copied him, he soon found his face growing hot and his breath labored. Still, the sense that everything from his neck up was floating in space was quite pleasant. When he swayed his head back and forth as if he was riding a wave, his father watched him like he was observing an unusual animal.

Presently, a woman in a kimono entered the room. She moved as if she were gliding, so the drunken Koujirou didn't notice her until she was right next to him. She sat down next to Koujirou and his father, who were facing each other, and bowed politely. His father glanced at the woman and nodded very slightly. Koujirou stared at her as if bewitched. Her white face was marred by a single scar, which made her look pitiful yet at the same time accentuated her beauty.

The woman who sat next to Koujirou and his father that day was Hanae, who would die mysteriously in their mansion two years later. That is to say, she was my father's mother and my grandfather's second wife.

○

Hanae married my grandfather and moved into the mansion several months after the day Uncle Koujirou drank alcohol for the first time. This alone was a surprise to my uncles, but an even greater surprise was the fact that she brought along a son who was already starting elementary school.

She had apparently been born in a town on the banks of Lake Biwa, but no one knew much about the past she had left behind on the far side of the Osaka Barrier, which demarcated the eastern boundary of the ancient capital. Of course, my grandfather and Kazuko must have known quite a bit, but my uncles weren't told anything, and her son, my father, knew surprisingly little about his own mother.

Needless to say, I never met Hanae. Although she was my grandmother, my image of her is frozen in time because she died when my father was a child. She is forever younger than my mother and will never grow old.

I saw a photograph of her once. There was something vaguely sad and cool about her. It was a group portrait of the family, so I couldn't make out her features in detail, only a vague impression.

○

My father smoked a cigarette and gazed out at the dim garden. Perhaps he was thinking about his mother. His feeble puffs of smoke scattered in the warm breeze from the veranda. There was still plenty of sake left, but the food they had brought in was almost gone.

Uncle Koujirou sat with his chin resting in his palm, his entire face and neck bright red.

"Hanae was a beautiful woman," he said. "Quiet and a little mysterious."

"I don't remember her ever getting mad at me," my father said.

"She wasn't the type of person who got mad. Of course, you were a quiet little kid, too."

Up till then, Kazuko had managed the entire household, and she didn't have the warmest of feelings toward Hanae when she first arrived. Since Kazuko was being so standoffish, my uncles treated Hanae and their new little brother with extra kindness.

"It took you a while to get used to us," Uncle Koujirou muttered, his chin still in his hand.

"Can you blame me?" my father asked, smiling wryly. "I was so much younger than you."

"I really looked out for you after Hanae died," Uncle Kouichirou said.

"You have my thanks," my father replied, bowing his head. Uncle Kouichirou pecked at the few remaining simmered vegetables with his chopsticks.

"I probably shouldn't say this," he said quietly. "But I feel like after Hanae died, you finally became a part of the family."

"Could be," my father said, nodding.

"We took you to all sorts of places. Remember?"

"Yeah, like the movies, and you showed me magic tricks, too, didn't you?"

"I did. I was obsessed with magic back then," Uncle Koujirou said nostalgically.

"Oh, and you once took me to a bar, too."

Uncle Kouichirou grinned.

"Dad hit the roof when I did that. He had a soft spot for you."

"Did he really?"

"Definitely. You might not have seen it, but he was soft on you."

My father smiled, not contradicting them.

"That reminds me, once when we were on our way back from a day out, you threw up. I had no idea what to do."

"I don't remember that," my father said, tilting his head and glancing at the altar. "Oh, look." The incense had run out.

"You did, I remember," Uncle Kouichirou said as he got out some more. He sounded astonished. "It was toward the end of the year Hanae died."

○

Kouichirou was home on vacation, going out on the town, helping Shigeo with his schoolwork, and generally taking it easy. Koujirou had gone home with a university friend who lived in Kyushu. He didn't plan to come back until New Year's Eve, which left Shigeo, Kouichirou, their father, and Kazuko alone in the house. Ever since that summer, when Hanae passed away, their father was frequently either out or shut up in his study. Kazuko was preparing to retire and move in with some relatives. Kouichirou was doing what he could to cheer Shigeo up. He took him rabbit hunting on Mount Yoshida and brought him along when he went downtown. He would make him laugh by telling stories about the crazy people he met at university.

The day Shigeo got sick, he and Kouichirou had gone to Shinkyogoku to see a movie.

At the time, Kouichirou was in the grip of an obsession with literature, and since they were in the city, he dragged Shigeo with him to several bookstores to buy some difficult translated novels. He liked to use the literary phrases he picked up in these books to bewilder Koujirou, who hated novels. To revive the flagging Shigeo, Kouichirou treated him to a bowl of udon.

On the way home, they stopped in Okazaki. They cut across the path leading to Heian Shrine and walked along the canal toward Nanzenji. Behind the temple, they could see the wintry forested mountainside, its fall leaves long faded. The muddy canal ran along to their left.

When they came to the boat dock, Shigeo suddenly squatted down. Kouichirou stopped walking, thinking his brother was tying his shoes, but instead Shigeo vomited loudly. Alarmed, Kouichirou squatted down next to him. Shigeo continued to heave several more times, one hand on the ground and his face white as a sheet. Steam rose from the vomit splattered on the street. This was enough to inspire panic even in the ever-cool-and-collected Kouichirou. He didn't know what to do. At any rate, he waited for the episode to subside, then cradled Shigeo up in his arms and ran to a tea stand next to Nanzenji Temple.

Someone from the shop brought Shigeo a cup of hot water, worried about his ashen face. Meanwhile, Kouichirou ran through all the possible causes in his mind. Had the air in the theater been bad? Had the used bookstore been too hot? Had they eaten something bad at the udon shop? He couldn't figure it out. Eventually, Shigeo picked up the little pickled plum the shop worker had brought him and took a sip of green tea. The color finally returned to his cheeks.

Kouichirou felt guilty for having dragged him all over the place.

○

Naojirou Higuchi dropped out of the canal project before it was done and promptly began a career as a businessman. Nobody knew why he suddenly started a business in a city he'd just moved to or how he raised the start-up funds at such a young age. I'd heard he cut off contact with the main branch of the family in Tokyo around that time, which didn't make him look any better.

The image I concocted of him in my mind was of an unpleasant young man with a razor-sharp mind who was incredibly daring and independent. That was also my impression of the Meiji period as a whole.

In 1897, Naojirou took up residence in the Shishigatani neighborhood. The mansion was remodeled over the years, so it wasn't exactly the same as back then, but apparently the six-tatami room on the north side, where my great-grandfather spent his last years and where Kazuko lived, remains virtually unchanged from a hundred years ago.

Naojirou eventually handed his business over to his son, but until the end of his long life, he never lost his powerful influence over those around him. He had a generous side to him, and there were always students and freeloaders around the house, as well as a stream of gallants, artists, and politicians. He often held parties at the mansion.

At the end of the Taisho period, Naojirou dazzled the neighbors with his grandest and strangest party yet. We don't know the details of that party. All we know is that during the war, my great-grandfather threw a party modeled on Naojirou's. The best we can do is use the fragmented images of my great-grandfather's party as a stepping-stone from which to extend the hand of our imagination toward the original.

After the fact, it was said that Naojirou entertained a god of death at that party.

Less than a month later, he went to an exhibit at the Takashimaya department store. On his way home, he collapsed on the grounds of Nanzenji Temple and died.

○

The year after Hanae passed away, as the weeping cherry tree in the garden scattered masses of petals, Kazuko moved in with her daughter's family in the city of Sakai, in Osaka Prefecture. Even as she departed the mansion where she had spent so many years, her stony expression held firm. She stood in front of the gate, turned toward the study on the second floor where my grandfather had shut himself up, and bowed her head.

She had looked after Kouichirou and Koujirou since they were children, and they felt it was quite unreasonable of her to be leaving when Shigeo was still so young. But it seemed that she and their father had already agreed upon everything.

Kouichirou and Koujirou accompanied her downtown, from which point she planned to go on alone to Osaka. They strolled through the gauzy spring weather talking about trivial old memories. As they walked along the canal in Okazaki, Kouichirou mentioned that this was where Shigeo had thrown up the previous winter.

Kazuko had planned to board her train at Shijo Kawaramachi, but instead she invited the two brothers to lunch. The three of them entered a restaurant in Kawaramachi. After they sat down, Kazuko's expression abruptly turned grim.

She asked if they had ever dreamed about drowning. They nodded. Her expression grew darker, and she asked whether, after these dreams, they had ever noticed a fishy smell on their body or felt as if someone was watching them. They didn't understand why, but she seemed to assign the utmost gravity to these questions. As she talked, her face became shadowed like a carving sinking to the bottom of a lake.

She didn't want to leave the mansion, she said, but she couldn't stand it any longer. Something was living there. She had sensed it when she first moved in, but it had gotten steadily worse after Hanae arrived. Kazuko often dreamed she was drowning, and when she awoke in the middle of the night, she would hear the sound of water. If she listened hard, she would begin to get the feeling that from deep at the bottom of a stagnant pool, some kind of strange creature was staring at her, and she simply couldn't stand it.

That was what she told them.

"It killed Hanae," she said, a tormented expression on her face. Kouichirou and Koujirou were shocked. But when they asked for more information, all she would say was that was how she felt.

The two brothers guessed she had gone into shock from Hanae's death and developed a nervous condition. The horror story she had just told them was not something the Kazuko they knew and trusted would say.

She told them to leave the mansion as soon as possible and live on their own.

The dim, inexpensive diner was noisy and packed with people, but Kouichirou and Koujirou were completely drawn into Kazuko's tale. She seemed embarrassed to be bringing them into her confidence about such a peculiar topic, yet at the same time, she seemed strangely elated. The brothers felt as if a strange chill had enveloped their little corner of the restaurant.

Kazuko departed Kyoto, leaving those bizarre words behind.

She never returned to the mansion.

○

This talk of dreams about drowning reminded me of something.

The old six-mat room on the north side of the house, the room where my great-grandfather had huddled like a burned-up pile of ash and where Kazuko had lived, was later turned into a storeroom.

Inside were several Japanese-style dressers and an old bookcase with double doors stuffed with novels and philosophy books Uncle Kouichirou had stockpiled in university. I often used to take books from its shelves and flip through them. I remember the smell of the stained old books and the feel of their soft, yellowed paper. Of course the content went straight over my elementary- or junior-high-age head, but whenever I found one of Uncle Kouichirou's faded underlines, I would read the text he'd marked. I don't remember much of what they said, but I recall his enthusiastic pen marks stretching out to the side of particularly dramatic excerpts.

Once when I was in elementary school, I was lying on the floor flipping through one of these old books when I must have become drowsy and dozed off. I heard a loud noise near my ear, as you might before falling into sleep paralysis, but it also sounded like a powerful, foaming rush of water. Overwhelmed by the sensation of drowning, I sat up, my mouth puckering open and closed like a goldfish.

The ceiling looked oddly bright. Stripes of flickering light covered its surface, as if I were lying at the bottom of a pool looking up. But I didn't know where the light was coming from. Feeling ill, I returned to the room where the rest of my family was.

○

The hands on the wall clock pointed to twelve. The chime rang.

Uncle Koujirou had fallen asleep, his thin back hunched. His white hair was disheveled, and his glasses were sliding down his nose. Uncle Kouichirou pointed at him and whispered, "He fell asleep!" Uncle Koujirou let out a groan of complaint, but his eyes showed no sign of opening.

Uncle Kouichirou's face was also completely red, and the beads of sweat on his forehead glistened under the fluorescent light. He pulled a white handkerchief from his pants pocket and wiped his face.

"Ugh!" Uncle Koujirou suddenly shouted.

"You woke up, eh?" Uncle Kouichirou said.

"I was awake the whole time," Uncle Koujirou said sulkily, then glanced up at the clock. His head was swaying faintly, and I could tell he was having a hard time focusing.

"Hey, it's after midnight. The people from the antique shop aren't here yet?"

"They might not be coming."

"Outrageous."

Uncle Koujirou stood up shakily. Panting, he planted his feet on the tatami mat and began to walk forward with wobbly steps. We started to panic, thinking he was going to crash straight into the altar, but at the last minute, he stopped and bowed to his father. Then he started moving toward the sliding screen.

"Are you all right?" my father asked his brother from behind.

"My throat is dry. I want some water."

"Me too. If there's some tea or something, bring it back with you," Uncle Kouichirou said.

Without indicating whether he'd registered that or not, Uncle Koujirou slipped out into the dark corridor.

"Think he's okay?"

"He's pretty drunk."

Uncle Kouichirou and my father sounded worried, but apparently it was too much trouble for them to stand up and follow him. We listened to Uncle Koujirou's uneven steps advance to the end of the corridor. My father lit a cigarette.

“Hair of the dog,” Uncle Kouichirou intoned, as if he’d just remembered.

“What are you talking about?” my father asked, blowing out a gust of smoke.

“Isn’t that what the heavy drinkers say, that you should drink alcohol to cure a hangover?”

“Did Dad used to say that?”

“No, Dad never said that, but before he died, all he’d drink was water. I just remembered that. I wonder if he was drinking off his hangover.”

“A lot of strange things happened, didn’t they? I guess the water was one of them,” my father said, as if lost in thought. “The grand party, too.”

“That’s still a mystery to me,” my uncle said, frowning.

○

My grandfather’s “grand party” took place at the beginning of July, with the rainy season still lingering. One night when Mr. Hisatani passed the mansion, he noticed bright lights bleeding into the quiet, lonely rain. Normally the lights would be out by that time of night, so Mr. Hisatani stopped, thinking it was odd. The mansion was glaringly bright but very quiet.

The next morning, when Misato came by, she discovered a large amount of leftover sake and catered Western-style food in the second-floor study. When she asked my grandfather about it, he said flatly that he didn’t know anything. She figured some relatives must have come over, but when she called to ask them, they said no one had visited that night. I remember her calling our house, too, and my father standing there with a puzzled look on his face.

Judging by the leftover food on the plates, the party must have been a lavish affair. It seemed impossible that my grandfather could have eaten all the food himself. In the celadon platter at the center of the oval table were the bones of a fish so large and well-formed, it could have been a scientific specimen. The other food had apparently been arranged around this dish.

Late the previous night, Mr. Hisatani had seen the mansion glowing brilliantly in the dark rain, and everyone thought quite a few people must have gathered in the study. But in the end, we had no idea who my grandfather entertained that night. It made my father and his brothers uneasy. The incident called to mind the grand party my great-grandfather had held in the midst of the war.

They asked Mr. Hisatani to tell them about this earlier party.

Large paper lanterns painted with strange pictures of frogs and catfish had been hung in the garden, and the mansion glowed with an obscene red light. Geisha with white cloth wrapped around their faces and a fortune-teller with a dragon tattoo were invited. Under the cover of darkness, men wearing *tengu* and fox masks came and went. Although we don't know the details, it seems my great-grandfather was re-creating the party his father Naojirou held at the end of the Taisho era. Far from a mere amusement, however, it was the catalyst for my great-grandfather's descent into deepening madness and isolation.

I wasn't sure if my grandfather's party was the next in this lineage. After all, while my great-grandfather's and Naojirou's parties were both garish and gaudy, my grandfather's was the epitome of quiet solitude.

Still, that party marked the point from which he was sucked ever closer to death. The glint in his eyes grew steadily more terrifying, and he would often fly into fits of anger that made things very difficult for my cousin Misato.

He often complained that he was thirsty. He stopped drinking alcohol and would drink only water. As Uncle Kouichirou had said, he brought to mind a man drinking water to sober himself up. It was like he was trying to consume the volume of Lake Biwa in an attempt to clear his head of all the alcohol he had drunk throughout his life.

○

In August of that year, I had visited my grandfather's mansion.

Just the walk from the bus stop through the house-lined streets was enough to coat my cheeks with sweat. I slipped into the mansion, fleeing the intense sunlight. It seemed much darker than usual. Misato came to greet me in the entryway and said my grandfather was napping.

She and I ate some ice cream in the dining room. It was the most modern room in the mansion, redone when Hanae moved in. Although it had no air-conditioning, it always felt cool. Perhaps it was the white tile floor. The long rectangular window looking out to the east was open to the screen, and I could see the languid afternoon sunlight outside.

"How's Granddad doing?" I asked.

"Not very well."

Misato was quite a bit older than me, but among my cousins, she was the friendliest. I remember her playing with me often when I was little. She liked to tease me with the magic tricks Uncle Koujirou had taught her.

As she licked her ice cream, she told me about my grandfather's party. We tried to figure out what had happened, but of course we got no further than my father and uncles had. She said she had been quite surprised to discover the remains of that dinner in the dim study. "I can't quite explain it, but I got the feeling there were a bunch of strangers in the house, and it gave me the creeps," she said.

I thought about how hard it must be for her, all alone with my grandfather in the big, empty mansion.

"You've got a hard job," I said.

"It's not so bad. I don't have anything else to do, after all. I owe it to my parents and my grandparents." She smiled but then added softly, "Sometimes, though, Granddad is so scary. It's not that I'm scared of him scolding me. It's this eerie kind of feeling."

"What do you mean?"

"Sometimes he mistakes me for Hanae, and it's just terrifying. Once he came up behind me in the corridor and wrapped his arms around me."

"But you and Hanae…," I said. She laughed.

"We're completely different, right? As soon as he saw my face, he came back to his senses."

The hardest thing, she said, was how he always wanted water.

No matter how many pitchers she filled and brought to him, he drank it all down instantly. And he always grumbled that the water tasted bad. Every day before she prepared dinner and went home, she filled two large bottles with store-bought water and left them in the study where he spent all his time, but when she returned the next morning, both bottles were always empty.

"I asked Dr. Yano about it," she said, then fell silent, listening to the humming of the cicadas outside. I finished my ice cream and drank some barley tea.

"A lot of other strange things have happened. Not just the party," she said. "Come with me."

We stood up. From the dining room, we passed down the corridor that circled the courtyard. When we reached the room to the north, I saw a glimmering light inside. I made a sound of surprise, and Misato nudged me into the room with a serious expression.

The large window to the west was gleaming white. The entire floor of the room was packed haphazardly with vessels of various sizes and shapes, all filled to the brim with water. The water was reflecting the light, making the inside of the room shine. The ceiling undulated softly like the surface of a pool. I felt as if the entire room had sunk to the bottom of a placid lake pierced by bright sunbeams.

Stunned and not thinking clearly, I stepped into the room. I walked carefully, making sure not to kick over any of the vessels. They were full of pure water. Not a speck of dust floated on their surfaces.

"When I got here this morning, it was like this," Misato said. "Granddad did it."

"Why?"

"Who knows?" she said, pressing her hands to her hips and sighing. "Maybe it's some kind of magic charm."

I looked up at the ceiling. I felt as if I had seen that quivering light before.

I stood there dumbfounded for a few minutes. Then suddenly, I noticed a small figure standing between the shrine and the bamboo thicket. For a few seconds, my heart pounded. But when I worked up the nerve to look more closely, I realized it was my grandfather. He was standing in the corridor across the courtyard, in front of the sliding screen, glaring at us with a frightening look in his eyes. Not long after that, his altar would be set up on the other side of that screen, and my father, his brothers, and I would be drinking together in front of it.

○

"As far as this family heirloom goes, it's not necessarily in the storehouse, is it? Have you considered the courtyard?" my father asked out of nowhere.

"Of course I considered that," Uncle Kouichirou answered, smiling cynically. "Dad called it our *guardian deity*, after all. But I couldn't very well dig holes all over a place he cared so much about."

"I can just imagine the uproar if you had."

"We could do it now."

"Let's see what Hourendou brings first."

"I guess you're right."

My father poured himself some sake and offered Uncle Kouichirou some as well. "No more for me," he said.

"I've always wondered about that shrine in the courtyard. What's it a shrine to anyway?"

"No idea," Uncle Kouichirou moaned, his eyes closed.

On the other side of the sliding screen behind the altar was the courtyard. Hardly anything was planted there other than some bamboo. Soft-looking green moss covered the ground, and when I was little, I'd always wanted to stroke that green carpet.

A little shrine was nestled against the bamboo. When I was young, I often watched through the glass doors of the corridor as my grandfather crossed the stepping-stones between patches of moss to place an offering at the shrine. Praying there, his features tense, he looked even more unapproachable than usual. Not much light reached the courtyard, and it was especially dim and chilly in the early morning, as if it were underwater. My grandfather would be standing out there, so close to me, but looking as if he were in some other world.

My grandfather hated for anyone to disturb his courtyard. Once, I witnessed him catch one of my cousins in there, staring at the shrine. Without a single word, he slapped him hard across the face. That cousin never came back to the mansion, right up until the wake. It made sense that my uncles had never dared investigate the courtyard, no matter how curious they were about the family heirloom.

"It supposedly hasn't been changed since the mansion was built," Uncle Kouichirou said.

"It's that old?" I asked.

"I heard Naojirou oversaw the transfer of the deity to the shrine. I saw Dad pray there so many times, but I never knew what deity he was praying to," he replied.

My father sat pensively for a moment, then said, "For some reason, I've never liked that courtyard."

○

I have a clear memory of my father telling me about mermaids when I was in high school. I remember it so well in part because he didn't usually tell stories that sounded like fairy tales, and in part because that hazy memory of a mermaid was tangled up with one of his few recollections of his mother. When I think of Hanae, a second, phantom image always floats up after, as if tied to the first by a string—a stalk of bamboo thrusting up from the indigo surface of the water and an old shrine decaying at the bottom of a pool.

We were visiting my grandfather's mansion during summer vacation. My father and I were sitting in the room on the west side of the first floor where our family always stayed. I think my mother had gone out shopping for dinner, since Misato was taking some time off. If we opened the sliding door separating our room from the corridor on the east side, we could see the courtyard. My father had brought two bottles of Calpis from the dining room, and we sipped at them as we looked out into the courtyard. The chirping of cicadas in the trees beside the storehouse drifted in through a window screen on the west side of the room. The sky was shadowy, threatening rain at any moment, and it was hot and humid. As we looked out at the shrine and bamboo grove in the courtyard, as dim as if they were submerged underwater, my father gradually began to speak.

His mother's hometown was on the southern edge of Lake Biwa. The little village was tucked into the mazelike foothills of the mountains that form the border with Kyoto Prefecture, just where they begin to stretch toward the banks of the lake. I don't know exactly where it was, but I think it was near Hamaotsu.

Hanae told my father about her hometown several times when he was very young. The hills on the west side, which led into the mountains, were covered with a large, dense grove of bamboo. If you walked through the bamboo grove, you would abruptly emerge at a pool. It was an eerie place, surrounded on all sides by thick stalks of tortoise-shell bamboo, leaning so far over the dark water that they looked about to fall in. For the most part, it was still and silent, without so much as the cawing of a crow. But on windy days, the sound of the bamboo stalks grazing one another echoed across the pool, and it seemed as if some enormous creature were writhing around under the water.

According to Hanae, a shrine surrounded by a bamboo grove lay at the bottom of the pool. Long before she was born, the villagers had done something terrible, and because of that, the god of water had sunk the shrine in the span of a single night. On that same night, a young couple happened to be meeting there under cover of darkness. The boy managed to escape, but the girl was swallowed up in the gushing water and drowned. The water was cold and dark, but if you dove to the bottom, you could still see the shrine, with the bamboo growing thick around it. The drowned girl had turned into a mermaid, swimming silently between the submerged stalks of bamboo. Hanae believed the girl must have become a human sacrifice to placate the water god's fury.

"I guess that story really spooked me as a kid, because I dreamed about it over and over." My father smiled wryly, sipping his Calpis. "I don't have that dream much anymore, but in the past, I had it all the time. I would fall into a dark pool. As I drowned, I opened my eyes and saw a mermaid swimming in front of me. When I thought back on it later, I felt sure the mermaid had my mother's face."

○

My father told the same story to Uncle Kouichirou.

"Now that you mention it, this courtyard does look like something out of that story," he said, nodding.

"But now that I'm really thinking about it, maybe I got it backward. Since I was looking out at that courtyard when my mother told me the story, it's possible I used what was in front of me while imagining the scenery she described."

"I guess. Anyway, it does seem like a story Hanae would tell."

Just then, we heard the loud sound of something heavy falling in the dark-wood-floored corridor.

All three of us jumped in surprise. We stared tensely at the sliding screen, but there were no more noises. The silence only seemed to deepen.

"Wonder what that was," Uncle Kouichirou whispered.

"Yeah, I wonder," my father echoed.

"Go see."

My father was drunk, too, and he tottered a bit as he passed in front of the altar. He slid open the screen and stuck his head into the corridor, then immediately let out a muffled cry and pulled his head back in. A second later, he shouted into the darkness, "Why are you standing over there? Are you trying to give me a heart attack?"

"Who is it? Koujirou?" Uncle Kouichirou asked, sounding bored.

"What's wrong?" my father asked, but Uncle Koujirou wouldn't come into the room. "Are you drunk or something?" he asked, stepping into the corridor. "Why are you looking at me like that?" Uncle Koujirou only groaned in response. "Hey, why is it so wet over here?" asked my father.

Uncle Kouichirou stayed sitting, sipping his sake and making no attempt to help.

"What a handful that guy is," he said.

I was just getting up to help when my father shoved Uncle Koujirou into the room, a dull, metallic teakettle and some cups in his hands. Uncle Koujirou looked at us searchingly, then glanced at the altar. He looked so creeped out that I felt a chill run down my own back. However, I didn't notice anything different about the altar. Uncle Koujirou hesitated, but when my father pushed his back, he finally came over to us. He sat down near the veranda.

"You still drunk? Sober up, man," Uncle Kouichirou said, slapping his brother's back.

"You sure gave me a shock," my father said, pouring some tea from the kettle into the cups. "Standing there in the dark with that crazy look on your face. I thought you were Dad's ghost."

Uncle Koujirou peered back at him.

○

Naojirou Higuchi had two sons and one daughter. His daughter married into a family in Sakai, and Kazuko was her granddaughter. His older son fell ill and died, and his younger son took over his business. That was my great-grandfather.

In Naojirou and my great-grandfather's day, the family business was a dyeing factory. Artists and scholars living in Kyoto often visited the second-floor study back then. My great-grandfather was a devoted antique collector who bought from various dealers. Eventually he strayed from the dyeing industry and began to dabble in Nishijin weaving, which caused various problems. The prohibitions on luxury items only made matters worse, crippling the Nishijin weaving industry and resulting in huge losses for my great-grandfather.

After that, he sank into a dark morass from which he could not extricate himself. It began with the bizarre "grand party" modeled on the one his father had held. Afterward, he would wander the paths between the rice paddies in Kitashirakawa, his obi sagging pitifully, or dive into the canal and have to be pulled out.

There were rumors that he bit off a piece of the ear of one of the artists who used to visit the mansion and that a monster he kept as a pet could be heard howling night after night. The distinguished figures who had once frequented the mansion stopped coming.

On top of all this, his obsession with antiques intensified, and he had never had much of an eye for the trade to begin with. He liked glass, carvings, and lacquerware, but above all, he sought out anything with a dragon motif. He couldn't say no to anything with a dragon, and once they caught wind of this, shady antique dealers began visiting the mansion. The storehouse was soon piled high with his haphazard collection. These were the items that were sold to Hourendou after his death.

When my uncles were in elementary school, my great-grandfather lived in a corner of the mansion. I don't know whether it was because he resented my grandfather for robbing him of his power or simply because he was weary of the world, but he stopped talking. His face was the color of ash, as if his long-neglected health and depression had coalesced into a solid mass. The fact that my young uncles were afraid to go near him only deepened his isolation and depression. He had been a heavy drinker, but once he was confined to the house, he was forbidden from drinking alcohol, so he drank green tea with lumps of sugar dissolved in it.

He crouched unmoving in the old six-mat room to the north, gazing out at the courtyard with his dark, cloudy eyes and sipping his sugary tea. That was the image of my great-grandfather etched in the memories of my uncles. He died before they advanced to junior high, as if he had simply melted away.

○

At the edge of the garden pond was an old-fashioned electric lamp in the style of a Meiji-era gaslight. My great-grandfather had it specially made before the war, when he was in the prime of his life, and it was still in use, albeit with some repairs. The post was carved with a dragon climbing toward the sky. Its light was weak, and it left pockets here and there where the darkness grew deeper. These pools of darkness seemed to be the source of the tepid breeze that was blowing into the room through the glass doors that opened onto the garden.

Uncle Koujirou had a strange look in his eyes. Meanwhile, Uncle Kouichirou changed the mosquito coil with unsteady hands.

"The water won't turn on," Uncle Koujirou muttered. "Wonder if the service was cut off."

"I didn't hear anything about that," Uncle Kouichirou said.

"How'd you make this tea?" my father asked, pouring a cup from the kettle.

"Misato must have left it for us. It was in the dining room."

"It smells kind of funny," my father said. "Maybe we shouldn't drink it."

"There must be some medicinal herbs in there," Uncle Kouichirou said without much thought.

The hands on the wall clock pointed to twelve thirty.

"I'm wasted," Uncle Kouichirou said, letting out a labored breath.

"What did you talk about while I was in the dining room?" Uncle Koujirou asked, his tone serious. "Were you talking about me?"

"I'd never talk about you behind your back, Jiro," my father said.

"Then what were you talking about?"

"Don't start a fight," Uncle Kouichirou snapped.

"I'm not trying to," Uncle Koujirou said. He shook his head

slowly, and his whole body swayed along with it. I could tell he was trying to gather the thoughts that had been scattered by the alcohol. "Didn't someone say, '*Drinks are wasted on that guy*'?" he moaned.

"Did we say that?"

"And then, '*He gets drunk so fast he can't even taste the alcohol.*'"

"We'd never say something like that!" Uncle Kouichirou said testily.

"I'm not saying you did."

"What are you talking about?"

"It was Dad's voice," Uncle Koujirou said, glancing at the altar.

"Listen to this drunkard. Dad's been dead this whole time," Uncle Kouichirou said.

"No, it was Dad. Do you think I'd mistake my own father's voice?"

"You must have mistaken one of our voices for his," my father said.

"But you just said you never said that."

"Stop talking nonsense. You sound like an idiot," Uncle Kouichirou said.

"You're drunk," my father added gently.

"Go out in the garden and sober up," Uncle Kouichirou ordered. His brother obediently stood up. He staggered over to the veranda and appeared to search for the clogs set out on the granite slab below. "Don't fall in the pond," Uncle Kouichirou joked.

"You think I could drown in a pond that pitiful?" Uncle Koujirou replied before stepping into the softly lit garden.

"What a creepy thing to say," Uncle Kouichirou said, scowling as he sipped his tea.

"But don't you feel some sort of presence?" my father asked, not looking at the altar but gesturing at it with his chin. "Wait, I take that back. *Presence* makes it sound too gentle. I feel like we're being glared at," he added quietly.

Uncle Kouichirou nodded reluctantly but did not look up at the altar.

Somehow the mansion's silence felt as if it were seeping into my body. My mother, aunts, and cousins should have been sleeping in the other rooms, but I couldn't sense them there. It felt like the four of us—my dad, his brothers, and I—had been left all alone in a corner of that sprawling, vacant mansion.

○

I went into the corridor. The passageway with its wooden floor was dark except for the faint stream of light from an electric lamp in the entryway shaped like an old-fashioned paper lantern. I tried to empty my mind and stave off any unnecessary imaginations.

The bathroom with its blue tiling was cool. I stared at the little frosted-glass window in front of me. When I was done, I flushed the toilet. But when I turned on the faucet to wash my hands, no water came out. I remembered my uncle asking if the water had been shut off. Yet when I came out of the bathroom, I could hear the sound of it falling somewhere.

I knew exactly what my father meant when he'd said he felt like we were being watched. Why did I feel that way?

I turned at the dining room and glanced into the darkness of the corridor winding around the courtyard. I considered going to my room and getting in bed, but I felt so unsettled, I doubted I'd be able to sleep.

In my mind, I traced the dim corridor through the mansion. Maybe it was because I could still hear water running, but I imagined that somewhere in the house was a dark, still pool. I remembered what Kazuko had said to my uncles the day she moved out. That something was lurking at the bottom of the water, watching us. The glint in its eyes was beast-like. It was delirious with fever, miserable with thirst, brimming with unrestrained anger at everything around it. It hurled whatever object was at hand. It craved water. Those fierce, wide-open eyes were the eyes of my grandfather on his sickbed. No—by that time, I believe my grandfather's eyes had become those of the thing at the bottom of the dark pool.

○

My grandfather, my great-grandfather's only son, survived a stint in Manchuria as an engineer officer, then after the war brought his wife and their two sons back to Japan. My great-grandfather's courage had failed by then, in part due to his business misfortunes and the death of his wife during the war. My grandfather locked him up, half insane, in a room in the mansion, and acted as his representative in the family business. The stories of my grandfather picking off the parasites who had prayed on his father reminded me of our progenitor, Naojirou. My grandfather closed the factory that our family had run since the 1800s and invited an acquaintance from Manchuria to help him launch a chemical plant. Uncle Kouichirou was currently running that business, and my father worked there as well.

When my uncles were in elementary school, their mother died, and Kazuko came to the mansion. Then, when they were in high school, Hanae arrived, bringing my father along to join the household.

○

When I returned to the room with the altar, no one was there. Surprised, I looked out at the garden and saw Uncle Kouichirou standing on the veranda smoking a cigarette, an absent look on his face. "Wasn't it there just a minute ago?" he asked in an irritated voice, looking toward the garden. I walked over to him and followed his gaze. My father and Uncle Koujirou were standing at the edge of the pond. I stepped into the garden. In the light of the electric lamp, something was writhing around in the pond with a squelching sound.

"The water's gone," my father said.

The stones covering the bottom of the pond were exposed. On top of them, several koi were flopping around, their scales still glistening with moisture. The gaudy colors of the fish only made the sight seem more cruel and unsettling.

"I wonder what happened," I said.

"The poor things. We have to do something," Uncle Koujirou moaned.

"Should we put water in a bucket and transfer them?" my father suggested.

"The faucets aren't working," I said.

"There might still be some water left in the toilet tank," my father ventured.

"That wouldn't be anywhere near enough. Let's put them in a

bucket and dump them in the canal down below. It's for the best," Uncle Koujirou said.

Although he had been drunk just a few minutes earlier, he now took charge and began to direct our efforts. I didn't like the feeling of the large, unfamiliar koi in my hands, but my uncle took his shirt off and grabbed them like it was nothing, dropping them into the bucket of water my father had brought. The fish struggled weakly in my uncle's arms. Uncle Kouichirou was frowning at us, but midway through the job, he grudgingly came over to help carry the fish.

After walking through the gate and down to the canal, my father said, "That's strange. I didn't notice that the water in the canal was so low. It's almost dry."

"There's never much water in there," Uncle Kouichirou said.

"Right, but now it would barely even cover my ankles."

"It's probably because we didn't have much rain this summer."

"You think that's it?"

There were around ten koi altogether, and getting them all into the canal was quite a job. It felt strange to be working so hard at such a task at my grandfather's wake. Still, I felt relieved that some of the weird tension that had been smoldering a little earlier had finally dissolved.

By the time we had finished and returned to the room with the altar, bringing the fishy smell with us, the hands of the wall clock were pointing to one thirty in the morning. Uncle Koujirou's pants were covered in mud, and while the rest of us weren't in quite such bad shape, our clothes were done for.

"We'll catch hell for this," Uncle Kouichirou said, grinning. Uncle Koujirou had taken his pants off and was using a handkerchief to wipe at the mud. "We can't even wash them," he said to no one in particular.

"I'm sure there was water in there earlier," Uncle Kouichirou said. "Or am I imagining things? No, I don't think so."

"There was definitely water in the pond. I remember someone stepping in it and shouting."

Uncle Kouichirou lit a new stick of incense.

○

Hanae died at the end of August.

My uncles remembered the day well.

It was a weekend, and in the morning, my grandfather took Hanae and Shigeo into the city. Kouichirou was leaving for Tokyo the following day, so he stayed home to pack up his things. Kazuko kept coming in and out of his room to check on him and help with this or that. Kouichirou was getting irritated, so he took a break. He escaped the mansion and headed for the university library where Koujirou had shut himself up. It was unbearably hot and boring there, so Kouichirou dragged his younger brother away from his desk and took him to see a movie.

There was a downpour while they were in the theater, and when they came out, the street was even more humid than before. They wandered around the city for a while and didn't get back to the mansion until evening. Tinted orange by the searing western sun, the house was eerily quiet. They stepped into the dark entryway, but Kazuko didn't answer their greeting. Hanae was nowhere to be seen, either.

When they went around to the room facing the garden, they found Shigeo sitting on the veranda by himself. Kouichirou asked him where Hanae and everyone else was. But Shigeo just kept staring vacantly into space. A powerful fishy smell was wafting over from the garden on the hot air. Kouichirou frowned. He walked around Shigeo and peered at his face. Although it was covered in beads of sweat so large they looked like water droplets, he made no move to wipe them off. Kouichirou squatted down next to Shigeo.

Koujirou walked farther down the hall and back to the corridor that circled the courtyard. It was slightly damp. When he reached the north side, he saw a woman with disheveled hair squatting in the shadowy corridor. It was Kazuko. A bucket was sitting next to her, and she was feverishly rubbing the floor with a rag. When he called out to her, she flinched as if she had just touched something disgusting, then turned toward him.

Koujirou returned, grimacing, to Kouichirou, who was squatting next to the silent Shigeo, at a loss for what to do. Koujirou said that Hanae seemed to have gotten into an accident. According to Kazuko, she had drowned in the bathtub and, just before they came back, had been rushed to the hospital. She said their father and Mr. Hisatani were with her.

Koujirou frowned at the heavy stench of fish in the garden. "What the hell is that smell?" he groaned. Kouichirou shrugged.

They were still crouching on the veranda when Mr. Hisatani returned from the hospital and poked his head into the room. "Did you hear?" he whispered. The two older brothers nodded. Mr. Hisatani beckoned to them, his expression somber. When they moved toward him, he cast a glance at Shigeo's small form on the veranda. "Ms. Hanae passed away," he said. "Where's Kazuko? And what's that smell?"

While Mr. Hisatani and Kazuko were talking, Kouichirou went out into the garden.

The bottom of the pond was bone-dry, illuminated under the western sun. The bodies of several dead koi were stuck to the bottom, their scales glaring in the evening light.

○

Perhaps because I had spent the night in the company of my grandfather's dead body and was fixated on ominous thoughts, something about Hanae's death didn't sit right with me.

My uncles hadn't been home that day. Only my grandfather, Hanae, Kazuko, and my young father had been there. Hanae had died. Kazuko was acting strange and later left my uncles with a bizarre warning. After the accident, my grandfather began to shut himself up in the study. My father wouldn't, or couldn't, speak about what had happened that day.

I looked quietly up at the altar. The fact that my grandfather was dead now didn't mean it was okay to concoct unfounded theories. But I couldn't help myself.

Kazuko had suggested that something was living in the mansion and that it had killed Hanae. Wasn't the thing living in the mansion my grandfather himself? I thought my uncles must have realized that, but I refused to say it out loud.

As I was lost in those thoughts, the fluorescent light began to flicker furiously, then winked out. We all froze. My own reaction was probably the most dramatic of all. I felt like my grandfather had read my thoughts.

The candles on the altar, now the only light in the room, threw our anxious faces into relief against the darkness. "What happened?" Uncle Koujirou muttered. "A blackout?"

Uncle Kouichirou looked at the electric lamp still glowing in the garden and shook his head.

"I don't think so. The bulb in here probably just went out."

"Now we really are playing one hundred stories," my father said, and my uncles exchanged glances.

"Wonder if Dad's going to come out of there soon," Uncle Koujirou moaned.

"Oh, stop being ridiculous," Uncle Kouichirou said, waving his hand dismissively. "Shigeo, there should be some spare bulbs in the cabinet under the stairs. Go get one, would you?"

My father tried to stand up but then glanced at the garden and bent backward slightly.

His face looked like he'd seen a ghost, so my uncles and I followed his gaze and all froze at once. A slender woman was standing against the faint lamplight. For a second, I thought of Hanae. I had never met her, but the woman in the garden had the softly sloping shoulders and fragile stance I remembered from her image in the photo.

In the flickering light of the candles, no one said a word.

Finally, the woman asked, "Mr. Higuchi? I'm here from Hourendou."

○

When the candlelight flickered, the darkness seemed to flicker, too. None of us said a word, as if overawed by the woman in the garden. However, she didn't regard us with suspicion and seemed completely calm. She embraced the small, cloth-wrapped box in her arms like it was a child she was soothing.

"Ah, the woman from Hourendou," Uncle Kouichirou finally said. "Please come in."

She bowed, removed her shoes, and glided into the room.

"You're quite late," Uncle Koujirou said. She simply smiled, making no excuses. The way she evaded the remark seemed almost ghostlike, and I found myself doubting whether she was really from the antique shop at all. It was odd for a young woman to have come alone at such a late hour.

In part because we were drunk, we all stared impolitely at her face, but she remained entirely unruffled. She began unwrapping the cloth bundle, revealing an old wooden box. As we watched with bated breath, she withdrew a strangely shaped object from the box and held it out to us.

"I'm sorry to have kept you waiting. This is the item you requested. Please check that everything is in order," she said.

My father and his brothers exchanged uncertain glances. At my father's urging, Uncle Kouichirou tilted his head and took the object. It was difficult to tell in the candlelight, but it appeared to be a strangely distorted sake bottle made of purple glass. Its two bulges were not lined up in parallel as normal but instead were twisted in relation to each other. A yellowed piece of Japanese paper fastened with several turns of sturdy twine covered the large stopper in its neck. When my uncle turned it in his hands, it made a soft sloshing sound. He handed it to Uncle Koujirou, who handed it to my father, who finally handed it to me. No one said a word.

The woman bowed her head and made as if she was going to leave, but Uncle Kouichirou anxiously stopped her.

"Wait a second. We have no idea what this is. What on earth is it?"

"It is the item we were charged with looking after."

"That's not what I meant," Uncle Kouichirou said, clearly

distressed. "What on earth is this strange glass sake bottle? Are you saying this is our family heirloom?"

The woman smiled and shook her head.

"No, that belonged to the previous owner of Hourendou. I was told I should give you the vessel along with the item we've been keeping for you."

"What do you mean? Whatever's inside this is our family heirloom?"

"I'm not sure. All I know is that the water inside belonged to Mr. Higuchi."

"This is water? Water?" Uncle Koujirou asked, shaking the bottle next to his ear.

"Yes. I was told that it's water," she said quietly. "Hundred-year-old water from Lake Biwa, I believe."

We listened, dumbfounded.

The family heirloom we had waited up for all night was water?

"Oh!" the woman suddenly cried, looking up as if surprised and staring out at the garden. She kept staring with narrowed eyes, so my father asked her what the matter was. She shook her head. "I thought it was rain, but..."

"It's not raining," Uncle Kouichirou said.

"I heard the sound of water," the woman said softly, listening to the garden.

I heard it, too. I could hear it falling into some deep, dark place, swirling and churning.

"Well, I'll be going now," she said, briskly rising to her feet.

We saw her off from the veranda. She stepped down into her shoes, turned toward us, and bowed her head. It was odd how each of her movements layered onto a mirage of Hanae in my mind. I glanced at my father, wondering if he was thinking the same thing, but his face only looked pale with shock. Uncle Kouichirou asked her if she'd be all right on the way back by herself. She answered casually that she would be fine. Maybe a car was waiting somewhere for her. I couldn't be sure.

"Wait, I have one more question," Uncle Kouichirou said. "You said someone called to tell you about the wake?"

"Yes, it was early this morning, around seven," she answered.

"What sort of person was it?"

"That's a difficult question," she said with a puzzled smile. "It was over the phone, so I'm not certain, but the voice sounded similar to all of yours. Only they sounded a bit older than you."

I thought it must have been my grandfather. But quickly I remembered that he had passed before dawn and dismissed the possibility.

After the woman left the garden and disappeared into darkness, it felt like she had never been there at all. We were left with only the water.

○

We placed the strange glass sake bottle and its contents in front of my grandfather's altar. Then we gazed at it solemnly in the flickering candlelight.

"Think it's water to cure a hangover?" Uncle Kouichirou asked abruptly.

"No idea," answered Uncle Koujirou. All the tension seemed to have left him. He sat down with his legs crossed and his shoulders slumped. "I feel like we were bewitched by a fox. That lady was creepy."

The clock hands were already pointing to two in the morning.

"Why don't you both get some rest?" my father said to his brothers.

"Not a bad idea," Uncle Kouichirou said absently. But something must have been bothering him, because he made no move to leave.

"What I still don't understand is who called Hourendou," he said, peering at the glass bottle.

"It couldn't have been Dad, right?" Uncle Koujirou asked hesitantly.

"Obviously not," Uncle Kouichirou declared. "He was already gone by then."

"It must have been Mr. Hisatani or Dr. Yano," I said.

"But they would have told us."

"Maybe they forgot."

"You think so?"

We were at a complete loss.

"Could it have been someone we don't know?" my father asked. "Maybe that's who he invited to the party."

We looked around, as if each of us was frightened by the others.

"It's like—" my father began.

I pictured the dark study on the second floor.

An image of my grandfather facing off across the long table with some kind of wet creature came into my mind. I could even see the water dripping onto the black table in vivid detail. But why did I imagine such a thing? It was because of the incessant sound of water and the image in my mind of those bizarre parties held by Naojirou and my great-grandfather. And finally, those rumors about my great-grandfather after his downfall—that a monster he kept at the mansion used to howl every night.

All of a sudden, Uncle Kouichirou hummed and tilted his head, listening. We listened, too. The sound of water in the distance had intensified. There was a bubbling sound and the rush of pouring water.

Sitting in that shadowy room lit only by candles, I felt exactly as if I were at the bottom of a dark shaft. As I listened to the sound of water from some undefined place, time seemed to slip back a hundred years to a canal construction site. Of course, I knew nothing of that time and place, so my mind merely conjured a vague image of somewhere cold, deep down in the dark earth. I was at the bottom of a long shaft. The shadows of the other men, drenched to the bone, writhed in the lamplight. I heard their groans. My body grew colder and colder. We had hit one of the water veins that sprawled sideways like some enormous monster, and no matter how much water we bailed out, it just kept gushing through the earth. Perhaps my great-grandfather's father, Naojirou Higuchi, was among those men.

"I thought the water was turned off," Uncle Kouichirou said angrily.

"Hey!" Uncle Koujirou suddenly shouted, giving us all a jolt. His eyes were peeled wide open, and he was pointing to the glass sake jar in front of the altar.

I brought my face closer and saw that the level of the water inside was slowly falling.

"There must be a hole in it." Uncle Kouichirou picked up the jar to inspect it, but there was no crack in the bottom, and neither was the area around it wet. Even as he held it, the water continued to disappear, as if some invisible person were drinking it down.

We held our breath and stared at the jar.

My uncle's words flitted across my mind: water to cure a hangover.

The sound of swirling water grew louder. I felt something cold on my backside and looked down. The tatami mat was wet. When I stood up, my uncles noticed, too. Water was pouring from the altar. Uncle Koujirou stood and started searching for the leak. He walked around to the back of the altar. Behind the closed sliding screen was the narrow corridor and then the courtyard. Suddenly, there was a sound like a stone being thrown at the screen, and several stains began to spread across it. My father looked taken aback. I heard my father let out a soft cry as he watched his brother from behind.

Uncle Koujirou opened the screen.

The courtyard was pitch-black, but the glass door was creaking as water spurted through its cracks like a flash flood. We half crouched, staring at the courtyard beyond the altar. Water shot through the darkness, pushing over the decorations on the altar. It poured onto the mats around us with a sound like palms slapping the floor. My father stood in the cold spray, staring out into the darkness of the courtyard. His face was white.

The water flooding the corridor through the cracks in the glass doors continued straight into the room, forcing us toward the garden. The water flew onto the altar and knocked over the candles, plunging us into darkness.

I thought I heard my mother and the rest of the family calling to us from far away.

As I stood in a daze before this barrage of water pouring out from the darkness, all sorts of memories and wild fantasies flew through my mind.

What Kazuko had said about something living in this mansion. The party my grandfather held at the end of his life. The bones of the large fish set on the inky-black table in the study. The pond that suddenly went dry. The glass vessels lined up in that room. The watery light flickering on the ceiling. The Lake Biwa Canal. The family heirloom that Naojirou Higuchi found. The shrine in the courtyard. Kazuko's question—had my uncles ever dreamed of drowning and woken up smelling of fish? It killed Hanae.

That summer, what had my grandfather drunk as he neared death?

Water.

○

Several months passed after the strange end to my grandfather's wake. The night the demolition of the mansion was completed, my father and I drank together.

He said it was difficult to make out the boundary between his real memories from early childhood and the products of his imagination and dreams.

In my father's memory, my grandfather opens the sliding screen.

My young father is standing beside him. Beyond the corridor and the glass door is the courtyard, but it seems darker than usual. The corridor on the far side is swaying. It isn't the courtyard my father is used to.

Brimming with water, it's like a huge aquarium. My father watches bits of moss and long, slender bamboo leaves drift across the sky. The bamboo thicket next to the shrine is writhing like a living creature. The glass door creaks, and water floods into the corridor. He glances up and sees the light hitting the surface of the water. He clings to my grandfather's large hand, but my grandfather remains standing, still and forbidding as a statue. There is a shadow of grief in his severe expression as he gazes at the submerged courtyard.

A fluttering kimono drifts across their field of vision. My father catches his breath. He pulls on my grandfather's hand, but my grandfather does not respond. He only staggers forward a step and then another. He reaches out his hand to touch the liquid spurting from the doors, and the water, reeking of fish, splatters my father's face. My young father retches.

A mermaid floats in the blue water, hiding between the swaying stalks of bamboo. The mermaid on the other side of the glass doors is my father's mother. She softly closes her eyes and seems to smile. Her face is peaceful, as if she is being embraced.

This is what my father remembers. As for what came after, he knows nothing.

○

The darkness in the courtyard was a swirling vortex. I could see uprooted stalks of bamboo rotating in the air, as if someone was swinging them around. A piece of wood from the demolished shrine broke through the glass door and came flying toward me.

The last candle flickered out, and our surroundings sunk into blackness.

The glass door made a cracking sound and flew off, and the sliding screen went next. Water flooded into the room. It crashed into the altar, then split into two torrents that rushed past us. The four of us clung to my grandfather's coffin, hunching over it.

A stalk of green bamboo pierced the back of the altar and hit Uncle Kouichirou in the face. Blood streamed from the gash, and I watched it dissipate into the flood of water. My uncle remained clinging to the coffin, scowling. Uncle Koujirou, too, held on to the coffin and bit his lip.

The torrent overflowing the courtyard grew in ferocity, as if it were trying to shake the entire mansion to pieces. Frowning through the spray, I looked over my shoulder. Beyond the mist was the garden lamp. The current cut across the garden, pushing its way among the trees to the street outside. I felt like we were standing in the middle of a water vein.

There, in that suffocating cocoon of darkness, amid the sound of water, I heard something roar. It sounded like the cry of an enormous animal. It was terrifying and filled with sorrow.

○

Late that night, the torrent gushing from the courtyard of my grandfather's mansion knocked over the wooden fence, flowed over the stone wall, and poured into the Lake Biwa Canal below. The water swelled in the canal and reversed course, heading for Lake Biwa. Foam swirled into whirlpools as the narrow waterway ran backward, sloshing over its sides as far away as the Philosopher's Path. The torrent ran from Eikando Temple in Shishigatani back to Nanzenji, shaking the brick aqueduct with an angry roar. When it reached the Keage Power Station, however, the torrent suddenly subsided, died down, and returned to its natural direction of flow. It never made it through the tunnels to reach Lake Biwa.

○

My grandfather had a sick bed made up in his study and spent his time there flitting in and out of consciousness. When my father or his brothers visited, he would invariably rise from his futon and greet them sitting on the shiny black sofa in the study, his sunken eyes ever more threatening. Often, they would sit silently, simply staring at one another.

The study was on the second floor and faced north, and it was as dim as the bottom of a lake. My grandfather's body odor permeated every corner of the dark, dusty room with its old vases and bookshelves. My father and his brothers couldn't stand to stay there for very long. What's more, if they visited too often, my grandfather would fly into a fit of rage. He allowed only Misato to look after him.

He said he wanted water to drink, so Misato filled a cup and brought it to him. He sat up, took a sip, and scowled, the water dribbling down his damp, twisted lips and onto the upturned cover of his futon.

"You expect me to drink this? It tastes like metal," he shouted, throwing the cup against the wall. Then he hunched over and groaned.

Misato placed her hand on his back. Beneath her palm, his gnarled, bony body squirmed like that of a lizard. When she saw his eyes peek out from behind strands of long, disheveled white hair, she jolted. They were not the eyes of my grandfather, ill and gasping. They were the strange, sparkling eyes of a beast, caught in a fatal trap but still struggling, desperately, to live.

"I won't die yet," my grandfather moaned. He repeated himself again, his breaths as hot as fire.

That was when he fell into a coma, and Dr. Yano and his son arrived, followed by my father and the rest of the family. By the early morning of the next day, he was dead.

○

The house that Naojirou Higuchi had built in the eastern foothills of Kyoto, that stood for so many years and survived several renovations, had reached its end. In early winter, Uncle Kouichirou arranged for demolition to begin. I joined my father and his brothers to witness the event.

After most of the splintered wood was carried off in trucks, we wandered around the empty property. It was strange how small the lot felt now that the sprawling mansion was gone. We passed through the vanished entryway, down the corridor of our imaginations, and emerged in the courtyard.

The mysterious shrine was already gone, and the broken wreckage of the bamboo grove protruded here and there through the muddy jumble of moss and rocks. A rusty, mud-covered lump of iron had risen to the surface, and a fat, twisted pipe stuck out of it, like the heart of a monster. It appeared to be part of a large machine, but it had been burst apart from the inside by a powerful force, leaving almost no trace of its original form.

We gathered around this piece of metal. Uncle Kouichirou looked cold with his chin buried in a navy scarf. Uncle Koujirou was wearing a thick sweater and smoking a cigarette. My father had his hands in the pockets of a mustard-colored jacket. I reached my hand out and touched the mud caking the cold iron.

My thoughts turned to the distant past. Once, there was a vein of water that blocked the digging of tunnels from Lake Biwa and caused hardships for the project's workers. Perhaps, I imagined, the hunk of iron in front of us was one of the steam pumps that had swallowed it up. And perhaps, on that late summer night, something that had been confined for a hundred years had broken free. It had ridden a current powerful enough to destroy my grandfather's mansion, but in the end, it had fallen short of Lake Biwa.

I slipped my hand into the warped curve of metal that had been pushed out from the inside. It was covered in smooth, round plates shaped like saucers.

"What are those?" Uncle Kouichirou asked, peering at them.

"They're beautiful," remarked Uncle Koujirou.

The plates were a translucent bluish color. When I held one up to the light and looked through, I could make out a soft rippling pattern. Through it, my father looked as if he were submerged underwater.

Those plates, faintly curved, seemed like horrifyingly large scales.